ALIENS ARE REAL

OLEANDER BLUME

WARNING THESE BOOKS ARE ABOUT ABUSE AND
CONTAIN TRIGGERING CONTENT

The Caring for Your Clown Series is about childhood trauma and
abuse and the process of healing from childhood trauma and abuse
and thus will depict instances and aftermath of traumatic events and
child abuse.
The types of trauma and abuses depicted, discussed or alluded to
include and are not limited to the following topics.

Physical abuse
Psychological abuse
Emotional abuse
Traumatic neglect
Child sexual abuse
Sexual assault
Miscarriage
Bullying
Transphobic rhetoric
Medical abuse
Negative self talk
Suicidal ideation
Panic attacks
Flashbacks
Anxiety
Death of loved ones

Please be advised that if any of these topics are triggering and/or
deeply discomforting, it is recommended to not engage in this
material.

Prologue

Snow danced in the sky, swirling in little flecks and flurries until they rested gently against the mahogany coffin that sat in the center of the somber gathering.

Oliver Tarsul stood at the front of the crowd, staring blankly at the box in quiet shock. There was no viewing, no dirge, and no remains to be buried with the casket.

All of this was a farcical attempt to provide closure to something that could never truly be closed.

Everyone here thought of it as a terribly sad day; it was meant to be a terribly sad day.

All Oliver felt though, was empty.

Six months later

"Okay, I'm heading out!" Oliver called as he readjusted the backpack on his shoulder and closed the screen door.

"Don't forget to feed the cats!" His step-dad, Jon, replied from the couch inside, watching something peculiar move in the treeline.

Oliver trudged around the porch toward the back and pulled open the five-gallon bucket of cat food, immediately alerting the pets of their breakfast.

All four of them swarmed at his feet, purring and meowing impatiently for their morning meal.

He obliged and poured the dry food into each of their bowls, nudging and picking up the slinky cats as they fought over which one would get food first. Not realizing they all had their own morsel.

"Bacon, stop trying to steal Pancake's food, your–" He picked up the brown cat and set it down in front of its bowl, just as another smaller black cat came to steal away from the aforementioned Pancake. "Gah– guys!"

Oliver scooped up the black cat but paused, his attention caught by something colorful at the base of the tree-line.

Whatever it was, it saw him too and promptly disappeared, garnering a look of aghast disbelief from him. *Must have been a trick of the light.* The beginnings of fall were an already peculiar time for the town, and people tended to see all sorts of weird things in the fog. Or go missing.

"Cats are fed!" Oliver hollered back inside, slowly turning away from the mysterious thing.

He began his trek toward the bus stop, discomfort slightly prickling his skin at the thought of being watched. Living well into the forest didn't really assist either; his and one other house were the only ones on the road. And he wasn't particularly fond of the kid who resided in it.

Still, he met up with the tall and relatively average-looking boy with curly brown hair, who casually waited at the edge of his overgrown driveway.

Douglass was the kind of kid Oliver had a very hard time being around. It wasn't his fault, he was just one of those people who think they're your friend merely by the fact that you're neighbors, and he never really seemed to catch on that Oliver tried very hard to not consider him anything more than just that. A neighbor.

Granted, it didn't help that he seemed so consistently keen on making sure he was 'okay'. He was fine. Really.

"Wow, summer really changed you."

"Yeah— it's called growth." Oliver grit his teeth, not exactly wanting to partake in the morning conversation. It was already getting chilly from the altitude, and he had somewhat hoped his cold shoulder would make Douglass stop talking altogether.

"I mean, you look good as a guy?"

"Don't mention it." Oliver sped up his pace, counting on the boy to get the message until his eyes caught sight of that same bright and colorful thing from before.

It stood just beside a tree, far enough that anyone not familiar wouldn't see, but close enough that the bright orange, puffy skirt stood out like a hunter's jacket. It was... *a clown?*

A lanky thing, pale as a piece of paper with a gaudy ensemble of mismatched bright colors, black and white striped arms, and a practically gravity-defying, double-pronged jester hat.

And it was staring straight at him.

"Do you see..?" Oliver slowed, craning his neck as he made eye contact with the clown before Douglass spoke up.

"See what?" His voice crashed through his head, loud enough that the mysterious entertainer also heard.

The thing took it as a cue to once again, pop out of existence. Making it just a little harder for Oliver to process. He shook the idea, the whole notion from his head as best he could.

"Nevermind."

He and Douglass climbed onto the bus, and despite the effort in body language, Douglass continued to pester him about the summer.

"So, I've been working at old lady Deauxtree's shop on the square," he said, utterly oblivious to Oliver ignoring him. "My dad doesn't know about it yet, but after Jojo passed, I figured he probably needed some help with stuff."

"Uhuh." He genuinely couldn't care less.
"He's working on this new project that's like, really eco friendly. You should see it. Hey, isn't your dad working on something too? I see the attic light on all the time, so I figured you knew about it?" *Blah blah blah.*

It wasn't important, so Oliver drowned it out with the nothingness of his own thoughts.

Occasionally they circled back to the random clown, but he was quick enough to think on other subjects. That is until the bus passed by what was an unabashed, seemingly deliberately closer, and exactly same clown.

Oliver's eyes widened and he pressed his face into the window, the colorful stalker stood quietly at the side of the road– *and no one seemed to notice!* Nothing aside from the normal chatter of children on a school bus at least.

It's obviously following me, but how?
It disappeared, completely– in a blink of an eye! It couldn't have been real, could it? My mind is messing with me.

He stared at it, and its flower petal painted eyes followed him, perfectly in time with the rolling bus. He even saw it as the bus drove away, still standing there, watching him creepily from the side of the road and no one seemed to care or even notice as it faded into the distance.

Oliver forced the thought out of his mind- he was just tired. That's all.

He went about his school day as regularly as he could manage. Still, the feeling of being watched unnerved him, and he couldn't help but occasionally glance out the window.

It was better than looking at his classmates, most of which were fairly gallful in staring at him without hesitation.

That in itself was enough to make him slump in his chair and doodle throughout the lecture on something about the pit and the pendulum being inaccurate to what actually occurred during the inquisition.

"Hey!" The voice pulled his attention from his furious little scribbles and toward the caller, she stood with her hands pushed inside her hoodie, glaring down at him from the other side of his desk as though he were some kind of abomination.

"Yeah?" Oliver grunted, glancing up before the familiar flash of color made him do a double-take. The clown stood outside the window, unceremoniously pressing its pasty face into the glass and staring at him. Oliver nearly fell out of his desk at the abrupt appearance.

"I don't know what you're thinking but-"

"I– I gotta go to the– the, uh." Oliver scrambled out of his seat, pulling it with him when he clambered over the rail. "The bathroom!"

"Hey!" The girl huffed angrily at his mildly polite and forced smile.

He was doing his best not to scream as it was and really, all he wanted was to not be followed by a clown of all things.

Oliver fixed his desk and promptly escaped the eyes of the mysterious and increasingly unsettling clown, though instead of going to the bathroom he tried to pace out his anxiety in the hall.

"Just..stop freaking out! It's just a clown." He tried to laugh it off, brushing his fingers through his sandy blond hair. "There's a lot worse things you can hallucinate."

Gathering his conviction, Oliver dragged in a calming breath before going back to class and turned to see the clown, no longer at what could have been considered a comfortable distance. Now, it stood less than arm's length in front of him with a dopey, bright smile like absolutely none of this was even slightly unsettling.

"Alright, I'm going to the counselor."

Perhaps it was pure shock, or maybe the growing

desensitization to whatever on earth was going on. But Oliver had finally begun to grow used to this random and consistent hallucination that bounced behind him as he walked toward the counselor's office, and a part of him hoped that it wouldn't follow him inside.

He opened the door, almost flinching when he saw the clown standing next to the oblivious counselor. "Mrs. Bradshaw, I'm being followed by an imaginary clown."

"An imaginary clown?" She thumbed through her papers and set them neatly inside a cabinet file. "Why do you say that?"

"Because it's standing right next to you, and I'm pretty sure it's not real." Oliver rounded her desk and fell back into the chair, watching the clown meander behind the counselor curiously.

Mrs. Bradshaw sat down at her desk and clicked her pen, not looking up when she addressed him.

"I know you've recently been put on new medications. Could it be a side effect?" She asked, half-mindedly flipping through his file. The clown leaned over her shoulder, before glancing up at Oliver with a large smile.

"That's...not how it works?" It wasn't a question but he couldn't help but be distracted by the clown as it pulled several balls out of seemingly nowhere and began juggling.

"Hmm..do you have a fear of clowns? Is the clown scary to you?" She questioned, still not noticing the subject of conversation while it moved on to balloon animals.

"No— it's…. a..normal looking clown." He dragged out the sentence, still trying to sort out what exactly was going on.

Mrs. Bradshaw finally looked up, prompting the clown to stop in the middle of nearly popping its balloon elephant and quickly stop existing altogether.

"Well, I can't legally do anything other than call your step-father and tell him of the situation. If you want to go home we have a shuttle?" She stacked the files and pushed it to the corner of her desk.

Oliver leaned forward, contemplating the idea. *It's probably stress, this whole thing is definitely stress. Another day off before school started for real couldn't hurt?*

"I'll take the shuttle," he answered.

The clown stopped being sinister and was more annoying than anything else. Completely quiet aside from the slight squeaking of its shoes when it walked, and its growing proximity to him, while it seemed to marvel at everything around it, treading on every last nerve of tolerance Oliver had left.

It was in the shuttle with him, leaning close to the window with shining stupid eyes, and it walked behind him on the way back from the bus stop, which felt ten times longer every time he heard that insufferable squeak.

"It's not real, it's not real, it's not real.." Oliver's mantra turned to irritation and quiet grumbling in his frustration at the quickening pace and closeness of what he currently and definitely considered the bane of his existence.

"The *cLoWn* is not *real*." He clenched his jaw, wringing the straps of his backpack tightly as the clown caught pace with him. If there was a more concise word to iterate this infuriating circumstance, he wouldn't have known it, but that didn't mean he wasn't searching for that word.

Oliver slowed to a halt, and the clown stopped too, looking stupidly confused at his slow descent into madness, despite being the unequivocal cause.

He whipped around. "Will you STOP following me?!"

That didn't work— if it had, it would have disappeared.

But no, that is too good of a thing to happen. Instead, the clown merely smiled the cheesiest little grin, almost like it was taking pleasure from his suffering.

Unbelievable, this isn't going to stop, is it? I'll just have to deal with a stupid clown hallucination for the rest of my life!

Oliver turned heel, letting out a nervous little laugh at the whole thing. *I really am nuts, huh?*

"I'm being stalked by a clown." He chuckled, almost actually finding it funny. He threw his hands in the air at the idea.

"I'm being stalked by a freaking clown!" Oliver exclaimed as if perhaps admitting the crazy notion might just make it end, or he could manage to cement it into the most absurd of realities.

"Alright, fine– it's great! This..is *great*." He pushed forward, distancing himself from the clown and sprinting toward his home, only to find that the freak had already been standing there on the porch waiting for him.

He huffed and let out an exasperated sigh of defeat before opening the door and informing his dad of the news that he was entirely insane.

"Oh, hey Ols, you're back pretty quick." Jon lowered his bowl of poorly cooked noodles and glanced up toward his son, seeing the colorful guest he brought with him. "I see you met the clown."

There was such a casual nature to his remark that Oliver wanted to punch the wall. Instead, he dropped his backpack to the ground and tore at his hair in sudden and painfully forced realization.

"IT'S REAL?!"

"Truly remarkable, isn't it?" The enthusiasm in his father's voice made his skin crawl at the idea.

A clown? Remarkable!?

Jon rounded the couch and casually approached the more or less unaffected stranger with child-like excitement, poking and prodding and going so far as to pull out a Geiger counter.

"Marie is the only person to have ever interacted with them, and she never recorded her findings." He mused, measuring the clown's height and width. "She would tell me all about them before– well... Your mom was a magnificent scientist. May I?"

His step-father addressed the clown briefly, gesturing for the silent and mildly confused thing to offer its hand and trying his best to ignore Oliver's discomfort at the mention of his mother. The alien creature obliged and the man promptly popped her arm clean off.

"Look at that! Ols, this is so interesting! It has no internal connective tissue, the entire body is made of– of some kind of semi colloidal substance covered in a film! Get the tubes for me will you?" He grinned, waving the clown's disconnected arm at his son and pointing it toward a heap of poorly kept test tubes and Petri dishes on the dining table. Oliver begrudgingly grabbed them, shaking off the shock from watching the disarming act.

"So how do we get rid of it?" The question seemed casual enough, though the bite in his voice proved a little otherwise.

Jon let go of the arm as it lost its form, becoming a grossly gelatinous substance as it returned to the clown's shoulder. "We're not getting rid of it. This is a huge discovery! Marie worked with them to build her portal, Mom-"

"Mom is gone because of that *thing*!" Oliver lashed, throwing a hateful glare at the alien thing and watching it's face paint slightly distort.

"This *thing* is the only way to get her back."

Jon's smile fell and his eyes grew stern.

His fists tightened before he forced a calming breath. "That's why she's staying. So I suggest you get used to her."

"Oh, so it's a *she* now?" Oliver huffed in disgruntled reply. *This is stupid, all of this is stupid! Does he not even think about my opinions? Bringing a mute alien freak thing into our house and just saying 'Oh, yeah this is your new roommate'.*

He shot another dagger stare at the clown before nodding grievously.

"Fine. But this isn't fair," he muttered, though his father was already hand waving the entire situation away in dismissal.

"You'll be friends in no time. You need some anyway," he replied as he walked off toward the attic, as though the words didn't slightly sting. Leaving Oliver alone with his stalkerish, silent clown.

He glared at her, readying himself for some kind of obtuse remark, or action that proved she wasn't clearly oblivious to whatever hellish situation she inadvertently placed him in. She did nothing though, aside from stare at him with a look that could only resemble some intrigue and recognition, like she had known him for several lifetimes but couldn't place exactly how.

"What?" Oliver bit, hoping she would do something, even if the prospect unnerved him. Her stillness was unnatural, in a way where someone who clearly doesn't need to breathe or even have muscles would be entirely still.

"God, you're a freak," he muttered under his breath, resolving to leave the alien instead of entertaining whatever idea she couldn't communicate.

He trudged up to his bedroom and shut the door, taking the opportunity of aloneness to contemplate the situation, whatever it was.

His eyes drifted toward a small photo on his nightstand.

It was a simple photo, taken at the art piece outside the AKAN lab; he and his dad stood next to the metal structure, and his mom sat on the ledge with her arm wrapped around him, squishing him into her side.

It was a good picture, taken just after his first treatment, and just two days before the accident.

She was gone after that. The state declared it an accidental death, there was a monumental lawsuit against the lab and his dad received millions in the settlement. The lab closed for a while. There was a funeral.

He thought it was just a fluke, that messing with particle physics would naturally lead to a nuclear explosion, or something close to one. It's what everyone said happened.

Encountering a Clown

Oliver stared a little longer at the photo, blinking those unwanted tears from his eyes before setting it down and turning toward his bed.

"CHEESE and crackers!" He gasped. Once again, the same stupid clown with her stupid face and stupid smile stared at him from somehow- inside his bed. Clipping through it like a badly developed video game.

Her grin dropped for a moment and some small look of artificial terror streaked across her face as though she were mimicking him, but quickly returned to that ostensibly quiet confusion.

"Are you enjoying this? Scaring the ever-loving crap out of me?! Don't you have something better to do?" Oliver grit his teeth, "like falling out the window or something?"

He glared back at the clown, catching some semblance of movement before she turned heel, walking toward his bay window and tipping backward through the glass.

"Wait–" Oliver gasped and his heart dropped to his feet.

He clambered over his bed to try and reach her before she phased through the screen, only to slam his knuckles hard against the glass instead. Oliver quickly threw the window open and peered down at what he could only imagine was going to be the splattered remains of clown guts. A deep dark part of him almost wanted her organs to be made of balloons and confetti.

However, that wasn't what he saw. To a surprising amount of relief, the– whatever she was– was entirely intact. No splatter whatsoever. She simply stood on the ground looking up at him with this face that screamed 'okay I did what you asked, be happy now?' Like a puppy dog expecting a treat for their trick.

Oliver let out a disgruntled sigh, and lumbered out of his room, down the stairs to confront her.

"That wasn't funny!" He spat, flailing his arm toward her. As if to gesture that the average thought process of deliberately falling through a window, was indeed as heinous as it sounded. Ignoring the fact that he had made the request.

Wasn't my fault she was that dumb.

"What were you thinking?! You can't just jump out a window because someone asks you to!" he yelled, his voice cracking slightly with his exasperation. "Are you really that stupid?! SAY SOMETHING!"

Oliver seethed, staring down the freak, feeling his face burn with rage at her.

This was on purpose. She did it on purpose, just to screw with me– how was I supposed to know she would actually go through the window. How was I supposed to know she'd actually be fine?!

And that ridiculous face, acting confused– scared, even.

"Come on! Talk!" He chided, scooping up a rock from the grass and throwing it at her feet. She dodged it effortlessly, removing her eyes from him to stare at the tiny weapon.

"Say something!" He held down his own vindictive laughter as he tossed another rock at her, plunging it through whatever freakish body she had and splattering black sparkling goo on the dirt. This time she flinched, her eyes darting back at him as her painted face wiled out in squiggling streaks, much like a cartoonish hyperbole.

"I know you can!" He spat angrily, rearing up to toss a good one and hitting her right smack in the nose with his last pebble, feeling pleased with himself for the good aim.

The clown's face contorted and twisted up in pain and his triumphant little grin dropped the moment she opened her mouth, letting out a painful, ear-wrenching metallic howl.

Her body collapsed into a swirling mass of darkness that blotted out any light that touched it, undulating and crying, lashing out at the grass, forming hands and claws and teeth, tentacles and tails as the abomination grappled with its form.

Oliver scrambled backward, tripping on his feet in terror. Tears bubbled in his eyes at the thought of what the monster might do in retaliation. *This is it. This would be my last moment before being killed or even eaten by whatever on god's green earth this thing is.*

He clenched his eyes shut, too terrified to see it, too afraid to move or scream or think. Until he felt a hand gently rest on his tightly balled fist.

"M-mom?" He trembled, his entire body wracked with the tension of tightening every last muscle he had. If he died, that's who he would want to take him away.

Another hand glided across his cheek, causing his eyes to flutter open. He sat on the ground, clinging to the grass and dirt, staring into the eyes of the clown.

She didn't look scary, or even angry— in that moment of small quiet, instead her brow furrowed in a way that showed unfounded concern. There was this calming air about her that reminded him so much of his mother that it hurt as much as it made him feel safe. "I'm sorry I scared you."

Oliver blinked. It was clear as day but the creature's mouth never once opened. It was like she reached into his head and whispered it with his own thoughts.

"Did you just—"

"I'm so sorry, I didn't—"

He wrenched his hand from under hers to hold himself in a moment of much-needed composure, cutting off whatever telepathic message the clown had.

"You can read my mind," He spoke in a hushed voice, still trying to gather his thoughts. The clown reached out once more and he jerked back.

"You– you can read people's minds?" He echoed the thought louder this time, looking back at her with bewilderment. She stared at him, her eyes flickering from side to side as she seemed to think of what to do next.

She situated herself comfortably on the dirt, maintaining some bit of distance before holding out a gloved hand and waiting patiently for him to do something.

Oliver hesitated, he glanced down at her hand and back up at her sympathetic face as she stared at him intently.

He reached out, pressing the tips of his fingers to hers, and immediately felt that same calming energy surround him like a soft blanket.

"Yes."

He snapped his hand back at the reply, staring at his fingers and wiggling them in confusion. His gaze turned to the clown, who hadn't moved an inch.

"Do..do you only do it by touching someone?" he questioned. The clown glanced down at her hand expectantly waiting for him, and he obliged.

"Yes," she answered. Oliver nodded and scooted just a little closer to prevent the cramp that was building up in his forearm.

"Can you talk at all without touching someone?" he asked aloud.

The alien paused, looking up at the sky as she thought.

"I don't know," she answered. It was such a strange feeling, he knew that it was his voice in his head saying these things, but at the same time, it wasn't.

"How does it work?"

"I'm not sure...I think– abstract thoughts?"

He wasn't entirely content with the answer– but it seemed to be final to the creature.

"Do you have a name?" *Probably should have asked this one first, but the concept of a telepathic clown overtakes common pleasantries.*

"Dindet," she answered, her eyes moved upward to meet him and he echoed the name aloud before following up with the real question.

"Why did you come here?"

"I think..." She hesitated, and static began to grow in his head, it wasn't his though, it must have been from her.

"You asked me to."

"Absolutely not."

If he hadn't already reached maximum capacity for alien shenanigans and cryptic stalker clowns from an unknown part of his mother's scientific past– this would be that moment.

It was already stressful enough dealing with the fallout, the funeral, transition, and school on top. He definitely didn't need or want a stupid clown with a stupid name talking through his thoughts, telling him that somehow— apparently, in a world he wasn't aware of, he asked her to come along to ruin his life even further.

Oliver pulled his hand back, stood up, and brushed the dirt from his clothes along with the preposterous idea.

"I never asked anyone to bring a freak like you here– I definitely didn't ask you personally, so leave me alone," he muttered, resuming his disgruntled frown and swiping his hand away from the miscreant's prying fingers when she reached for him again.

"Don't touch me." He shot. "Talk like a person or go screw with someone else."

Dindet lowered her hand with a somewhat somber pause before that cheeky grin slipped across her face, which only served to annoy Oliver further.

"I'm not a person!" The voice was loud and clear in his head, causing him to whip around, removing whatever contact caused him to hear it.

The clown giggled in his head, donning a sly little grin as she pointed at his shadow.

It wasn't a shadow though, it was an extension of whatever she was, sliding right under him.

"Stop that!" Oliver lifted his feet, pulling the gelatin with him. It didn't feel like any particular type of substance– like liquefied air or maybe glue.

"Stop what?" she asked, though he knew there was a hint of a joke in her tone.

"Touching me! It's gross– you're gross!" He kicked his heels against the dirt to push the goop off, instead it separated into perfect little beads that connected to each other in a sticky, unwanted ankle bracelet.

"Please teach me?" The question was earnest enough to give Oliver a moment of pause from his half-balanced, one-legged attempt at tearing off the accessory.

"What? To talk? No! Figure it out on your own! get– get this thing off me!" He stumbled, just as his middle finger wedged itself in between the now solid bracelet. He twisted in an attempt to stay upright while the freak of nature casually walked around him with a more than unnecessary look of amusement on her face.

"If you promise to teach me, I'll remove it." She pointed silently at the hexagonal house arrest. "If you don't I can make it heavier." With a slight wiggle of her finger, the bracelet packed itself densely around his ankle, the weight of it offsetting whatever balance he had left and forcing him to topple over into the dirt again. "Okay, okay fine, I'll teach you!"

***

Oliver begrudgingly sat on his bed, staring down at the heavy bracelet around his ankle. He shot a glare at the cause that sat eagerly in front of him while he flipped through his biology book.

"Do you really have to leave it on?" He huffed, turning to the human anatomy section to try and figure out what exactly constitutes as essential for speech.

"I can't say anything to you without it. So for now, it stays." Personally, he would have rather tuned her out entirely but she, for some God-forsaken reason, thought the best way to keep him on track was to start screaming terrible improv songs into his head.

"How did you make that shrieking noise earlier?" Oliver questioned, trying to find some kind of connection between that and talking. It was the closest thing he had at the moment. "That's kind of like talking right?"

Dindet put her finger to her chin in contemplation of the idea, before answering.

"I think I did this."

The clown repositioned herself slightly and smiled, and a horrendous, piercing cry, like two icebergs, slowly rubbing against one another, emanated from her entire body so loudly that it shook the foundation of the house.

"OKAY STOP!" Oliver howled, cupping his ears.

Dindet's screeching stopped, followed shortly by thundering steps down the hall and the door being swung open by his dad.

"Is everything alright?!" Jon huffed, half out of breath, his eyes flickering from his son to the clown and back. "What on earth are you doing?"

"Trying to teach her words," he replied, rubbing his ears to help pop them.

Jon straightened up a little and collected himself, fixing his collar.

"Right, see? I knew you could get along." He smirked with a nod causing his son to grow flush at the notion.

"She put a cuff on me!" Oliver retorted, lifting his leg to show off the proof of his detainment.

"That's great, Ols," Jon remarked, no longer listening, as he was already halfway up the stairs. Oliver let out a mild huff of dismay before turning back to his anatomy book.

"Okay, how did you do that?" He grumbled, turning the page to the intestines.

"I don't know."

Seriously? How do you not know how you make noise but know how to telepathically talk to someone.

"Are you really that stupid?" Oliver gawked at her, baffled by her complete naivety concerning her own species. "Were you born yesterday or something?"

"Yes!"

Oliver stopped himself and lifted his head to stare at the clown.

"You're serious." There was little chance she wasn't. Honestly, he didn't really know what to believe. Dindet nodded gleefully like it was a genuine compliment.

"Why does that make so much sense?" He whispered under his breath before turning the book around to show the alien what he had found.

"You're supposed to have these, every person has them and we use them to breathe, they are called lungs."

Oliver pointed at the diagram to show her where they were, then trailed his finger up to the vocal cords and esophagus.

"We also have these, we use these to talk and sing, and my mouth and nose–" he pointed to his own face this time, demonstrating the action of breathing through each at a time. "The holes are where the air goes in, down the windpipe, and into the lungs. And it all together makes me able to talk with vibrations."

"I don't have any of those," Dindet said softly, reaching at the book to grab a better view.

"Right." Oliver nodded, "because you're not a person."

"I think.." He hesitated at the idea, not really wanting to risk his eardrums, but also greatly preferring that over her nonstop static in his head. "I think if you do that shriek thing but instead try to make words, you can learn to talk."

"Really?!" The static cut away with her enthusiasm at the idea and she bounced lightly on the bed.

"Yeah- uh, try saying something out loud?"

"Like what?"

"Anything," He sighed, searching his room for something simple enough to say. His eye caught a photo he had taken of the sunset last summer. *Photo...good enough.*

"Say photo."

"Photo."

Oliver rolled his eyes. "Not in my head, say it out loud. It doesn't work if you say it in my head."

"I can't," she replied, once more in his head. The static around her intrusive thought grew a little louder in her followed silence.

"Why not?" he replied incredulously, causing the static to further increase until a soft thought interrupted.

"I don't know your language."

"How do you not know my language?! You're talking to me in it, in my own head!" he exclaimed, getting more and more fed up with the effort. Dindet's face streaked with mirrored anger at his words, if only for a short moment.

"I'm using your knowledge– not mine!" she retorted, "I can't say what I don't know."

"Alright." Oliver threw up his hands in defeat and slid off the bed. "Fine."

He moved over toward a shelf full of knick-knacks and old

books, pulling out a dictionary and tossing it at the clown.

"I don't care how you do it, osmosis or whatever– just learn." He grumbled, trudging down the stairs to the living area to turn on something that would occupy his mind other than babysitting a stupid alien clown.

This whole thing was a waste of time.

Oliver flopped down on the couch and fiddled with the remote, trying to find something to watch. Anything that would drown out the noise of his parasitic house guest.

It was like she had nothing in her head at all times, just this god-awful noise that permeated everything like tinnitus, but slightly worse.

He flipped the channel to an old sitcom, preferring the laugh track over the other noises. Some show about friends or the like- it didn't matter.

He simply wanted to be rid of the freak for a moment long enough to not explode.

How do you not know anything about what you are? What you are made of? If you can be born in a day and not even have to be a baby and grow up, or learn to walk, how can you possibly be so ridiculously dumb at the same time?

He felt a little bad at the thought. He didn't really do anything to help with that. *It's not like she had anyone to raise her. Could she even have parents?*

The thought was like salt on a fresh wound- no mom or dad. *No way to even talk to anyone. No one to protect you when things got bad. Or when someone was going to take you and-*

Maybe I should actually try to help.

***

Dindet stared at the open dictionary, trying to make something of the squiggles and symbols that she recognized through repetition, but nevertheless, couldn't understand. She tried though, hard as she could until something in the corner of her eye caught her attention.

A piece of glass, clamped against a wooden frame that held a tiny still memory. The alien crawled over the bed and stood up to inspect it further, it had the boy she was here with and the man. And someone else.

Dindet drew the photo closer, drinking in every detail of the image, something about it was familiar in a way she couldn't yet comprehend, and as she stared at it, she felt like the dimension she stood in had tilted slightly.

~~That's not right.~~

Her attention flickered though, very briefly to some folded-up piece of paper shoved unceremoniously under the boy's alarm clock, with big red letters on it that she couldn't understand. She reached down and tugged at it, unfurling the thin slice, until the big letters on it were far easier to see.

"What are you doing?" Oliver's voice came from the doorway, interrupting her moment of solitude. There was a genuine look of concern in his eyes for the smallest of seconds before it was quickly replaced with annoyance and a rage that Dindet could palpably taste.

"Don't touch that." The sternness of his voice prompted her to immediately set the paper down but before she could, he snatched it out of her hands and shoved her back. Forcing the alien to ripple in effort to remain intact.

"You're scared." She interrupted his thoughts quietly.

Oliver's scowl dropped and for a second, he forgot that she couldn't actually read.

Something was different about the clown now, like that silly, close to annoyingly contagious joy was sucked away. Or perhaps it was her silence coupled with the noise in his mind that he had a feeling only came from her.

"It's not important," he answered, folding the court order back into a tiny square and shoving it deep into his pocket.

"What is it?"

"I told you, it's not important, and it's none of your business anyways." Oliver shooed her away, knowing that it probably wasn't going to work. It didn't.

Dindet dipped around his bed, leaning a tad too close to him as if she were trying to read something over his shoulder, even though nothing was really there. "Then why are you scared?"

"I'm not."

"You're lying."

"Do you want help?" He promptly evaded. *What a glorious way to phrase it, Ols, do you want help– of course, she wants help why not say something smart like 'I'm sorry I threw rocks at you and called you a freak'– do you want help.*

She didn't answer in his head, or if she did he didn't hear it. Instead, she bowed her head in a nod, and stepped away from him, sitting neatly back on his bed.

Oliver plopped down too and leaned back to grab the dictionary he'd thrown her earlier, hoping to distract her with stupid words so she wouldn't go digging through his stuff like a creep.

"So first, I'll show you the alphabet."

Clowning Around

"Brown quick the...the jump, o-over?" Dindet moved her mouth, or what could technically be considered one, in an attempt to say the simple sentence.

Oliver pressed his fingers to the bridge of his nose in an effort to release the tension that had been built up after a decent four hours of trying to get a creature with no organs or functioning vocal cords to enunciate the English language with some degree of intelligibility.

"Alright...that's good enough." It really wasn't. She was horrid, misplacing verbs and nouns and pronouns with little regard for whatever gibberish was actually coming out of her mouth. Even then, she wasn't using what could have conventionally been called a mouth. So trying to teach the clown to move what looked like a mouth- and wasn't one- while simultaneously iterating whatever she meant to say was a logistical nightmare that Oliver, in all his creative ability, could barely navigate.

However, one thing that Dindet had more or less nailed down with efficiency was simply stating, 'Hello, my name is Dindet'.

Oliver set the useless dictionary aside and gestured for the alien to remain seated as he stood up.

"I'm going to show Dad, stay here, don't touch anything," he stated, walking backward toward his door, making sure to keep as much eye contact with the vanishing little devil for as long as he possibly could.

The clown stared at him patiently, entirely still as he slowly crept through the door until she was almost out of sight.

"Dad! I taught the clown to talk!" He called up toward the attic. No reply.

Must be something important.

He made his way up the stairs, listening closely as the sound of chalk on a board grew louder alongside his father's murmuring.

"Dad, I taught the clown to..." Oliver trailed into silence as he pushed the door open revealing a monstrosity of a makeshift laboratory.

A large mechanical platform contraption sat in the center of the attic, surrounded by cages upon cages of screeching mice. Blueprints and notes were strewn across foldable tables that created a maze of trip hazards all around the unfinished machine and the chalkboard that his father was entirely engrossed in.

The man spun around dizzily, searching for something on one of his tables. He staggered to grab a vial of the sample he had taken from their surprise guest and dropped some other substance inside that caused a small reaction, which subsided in an instant.

"Dad," Oliver repeated, "DAD!"

Jon popped his head out from behind the chalkboard in startled confusion.

"Oh, Oliver! Look– look at this!" He stumbled around the board, flipping it to face him and show off the chemical structures he'd discovered within the past few hours. "I- I've been testing this sample of the clown– because for some reason she has an incredibly high level of radiation, near lethal!"

He was excited, more excited than Oliver had ever seen before, his father never stuttered unless he was incredibly excited. It was almost as bad as the day he proposed to his mom.

"But, but, but– you see, there's something countering these, these high levels of radiation, look." Jon thrust a glass jar into his son's hands and quickly pointed toward his board, which had scribble after scribble of molecular structures. All but a few labeled with representative elements of the periodic table.

"I found each and every element on the periodic table, including the most deadly, and about 24 traces of base substances we haven't even discovered!" The man was ecstatic, erratic, spouting away chemistry nomenclature only he could understand. Oliver blinked in quiet astonishment, despite having little to no understanding of what was being talked about, the sheer joy his father radiated proved that he made a breakthrough.

"Don't you see?" Jon wrapped his child in a strong bear hug before setting him down and looking directly at him, giving away the several hours of nonstop work that turned the circles under his eyes dark. "Whatever that thing is, its entire makeup is a-a- a god particle!"

"I taught her to talk," Oliver replied, pushing the sample back toward his dad.

"You- you taught it– her to talk," Jon repeated half-mindedly before the realization of it dawned on him.

"You taught her to talk?! What can she say, can she tell us her compositional makeup? How does she breathe, move? Does she have any organs?" He was rambling again.

"Dad, she can only say like, one thing. Out loud." Oliver replied, stepping around his pacing father in an effort to direct him to his own scientific endeavor.

"Right, right, go ahead, let's see." Jon strode forward ahead of the boy, making a b-line for his room.

"Okay." Oliver hesitated at his bedroom door, praying that the clown wasn't wrecking his entire room in the few minutes he wasn't staring at her. "Don't get your hopes up, it's not that impressive."

Oliver pushed through the door, wincing just in case, but the clown still sat entirely motionless, as if waiting patiently to perform for the meager audience.

"Okay, do your thing." He directed with a weak gesture. Dindet nodded and stood up to fully face Jon, donning a bright smile.

"HELLO, MY NAME IS DINDET!" She bellowed, loudly enough that she shook the knick-knacks on his shelves.

Oliver let out a beleaguered sigh, "You did it too loud–"

"That's extraordinary!" His father cut him off, pouncing on the scientific opportunity presented. "How on earth did you do that? Some kind of fine-tuned vibrational training?! And so fast!"

Oliver trailed behind his father. *She didn't even do it right, and he is praising her? I taught her!*

"Ols, you're a genius!" Jon glanced back with an enthusiastic grin, beckoning him forward to look at the specimen. "It doesn't have any vocal cords or organs, and you somehow taught it to use this- this matter it's comprised of to speak English! Not only that, but it perfectly mimicked the movements of the human mouth!"

"I mean, I guess it's pretty cool." Not an entirely hollow remark, he had spent hours after all. "She can also read minds."

"She can *what?*" Jon bolted upright at the idea, turning back toward his son for confirmation.

"It's really weird though, like thinking with your thoughts or something," he explained, hoping that it made enough sense.

"Remarkable!" Jon turned back to the alien in the room. "Will you talk to me?"

There was little comprehension to be made from the clown, aside from the intent stare the man had, recalling which words meant what was sadly a loss on Dindet entirely.

"You gotta like, hold hands or something," Oliver grumbled, it felt like the cheesiest, most scifi thing he'd ever said.

"Oh. Oh! Okay." Jon gently reached out his hand as if to shake Dindet's and waited for her to comply.

The clown looked down at the hand in confusion, glancing up toward Oliver to garner some kind of permission, he didn't like her talking to him— how exactly was she supposed to know that the other one wasn't the same?

She hesitated but took the man's hand just as well.

He tasted like grief and sorrow, desperation, a shockingly painful and resonate feeling that immediately short-circuited her entire thought process.

It was delicious in a way that she only vaguely understood.

Unpleasant. I don't like this. Marie.

Marie? Who is that.

I want her back, please, please, please come back to me. I need you, we need you. We miss you.

It's your fault, isn't it.

You know it is.

You and your kind took her from me, I hate you, loathe you. Abomination. I'll dissect every last inch of you until there's nothing left.

No... she made me.

"I'm, I'm not hearing anything." The words broke the noise and screaming— red and hot cinnamon tart hatred.

"It's just static, isn't it?" The other voice said. *How can a single room be so full of hatred and anger? The room was wrong in every way, this is wrong.*

Something's wrong.

I need to leave.

It was less than a blink when Oliver noticed that his father wasn't even near the clown. She had completely vanished.

In the void between voids, that's where she went, but the two of them didn't know that. It had proven to be useful in the past to escape things that didn't like her so it seemed more than pertinent at the moment.

Why did everything hate her so much? The boy was the one who asked her to come. Right?

The memory was burned in her head like a fresh branding.

It was the only thing she knew above ~~everything and all the sideways~~

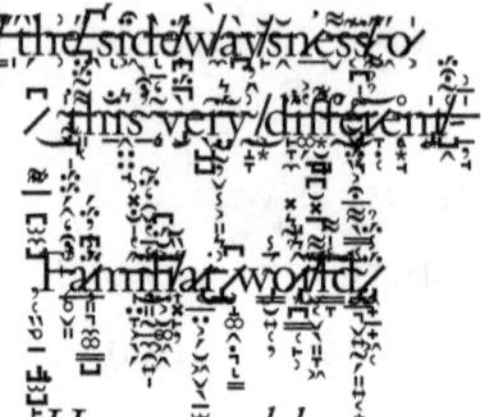

He wanted her to come here, so why is she still hated? What did she do wrong?

She said words like he asked, and went through the window. She must have done something wrong.

That's okay. She could come back later- maybe it would taste better after a few minutes.

Things won't be so ~~tilted.~~

***

"Dad..she's gone." Oliver blinked, she was just there, and then she disappeared. Again.

Honestly good riddance.

"I realize that son," he replied, getting up from his kneeled position. "We have to find her."

"What? Why?" Oliver followed his father as he quickly moved up the stairs toward the attic, stopping every once in a while to make a quiet mental note.

"She's our only way to get back Mom," he answered deafly, extracting a small glob of his sample and setting it in some kind of machine. "And also a major scientific discovery to the entire human race, luckily-"

Jon spun around, shaking his Geiger counter with a knowing little smile. "She's highly radioactive."

"Okay, but do we really need her?" Oliver argued.

"I'd say good riddance.." he answered himself under his breath.

All of this effort over a freak clown that can't even talk, or read— what could it possibly contribute to finding Mom? It's her fault she's gone in the first place.

"Get in the car, bring a jacket." Jon directed as he swiftly made his way toward the door, stopping by the kitchen to grab a snack for the ride.

The scientist personally couldn't quite understand why the clown would disappear like that, he had tried to be as respectful as possible.

However, he did not know even the deepest of thoughts are not protected by her veracity.

"Do we really-"

"Yes! Oliver," Jon snapped, causing his son to quiet, "If anyone at the lab finds her, or any of our equipment spikes, we will lose our chance. You won't see— we....won't see her ever again."

***

Rather than remaining by the tall and small humans, Dindet decided to better spend her time elsewhere in hopes that the unpleasant flavor of disgust would wear off in some amount of time.

After all, she had never been in a place before, around other intelligent creatures, and never in a moment so long and quiet as this one. It was peaceful and safe. They wouldn't find her here.

The clown pressed through time and space, finding herself back from the void between it all. It was brisk and cold, enough that if she stood still too long she could probably reach some type of freezing point.

Other humans strolled along a somewhat busy street, stopping every once in a while at buildings with colorful signs she didn't understand in the slightest. Well— that was something of a small lie, the particularly simple words were readable.

People occasionally stopped in their tracks at the sight of her, but never with the same stench of distaste as the other two had.

"Hello, dear, are you lost?" The voice caught her attention, and Dindet turned toward a much wrinklier version of a human being. She was hunched slightly forward with several stones on her wringing fingers and a permeation of genuine concern.

"Hello, my name is Dindet," she replied, hoping that it would suffice for the time being.

"Hello, Dindet, you seem to be new around here, are your parents nearby?"

That meant something, right? What were the important words Oliver said? Cars are important. Uh, something called a 'mom'? He thought about that a lot.

"Mm...mom?"

"Oh, I understand. Here, here, come sit with me in my shop." The stranger beckoned her toward a small cramped building with barely enough in-between space to hide inside.

Smaller, not breathing humans sat in perfect rows next to each other in various states of decay. Old things covered in rust and a significant amount of knobs and keys with strings and paper covered in numbers were strewn about wooden carved boxes and drawers, and dressers with fabrics that yellowed after years of wear.

"Have a seat, dear." The elderly woman gestured toward a stool for the clown to sit at, and she abided, hopping onto the stool and immediately realizing that the entire thing could spin.

"Just stay right there and I will make a few calls." The shop owner mused, and slowly waddled into the back of the store. "Douglass dear, can you move the donations away from the liftgate? The boys are coming by to pick them up tomorrow!"

The clown twisted around in her stool to face the back part of the shop. The wrinkly person gestured at some other person, a boy about the same height as Oliver, but with much curlier hair and an overwhelming flavor of compassion.

He nodded at the old woman and promptly began picking up boxes, dropping in and out of sight as he moved behind the shelves.

This is nice, she imagined, something about all the old things here brought a sense of calm that she secretly, desperately wanted. She could stay here for a while maybe. Since no one else wanted her, and the wrinkly one was kind without that quiet loathing.

Dindet's eyes trailed around the inner workings of the store, each toy and knick-knack was deliberately set in places that seemed unorthodox but pleasant all the same. Like all the ones in Oliver's room. The most ornate toys tended to draw her attention.

A peculiar-looking box that was shaped somewhat like a tent and made of aluminum that had rusted for a few years at least, was the thing her curiosity returned to most often. *The lady told her to sit though.*

Sit here…wait. Maybe ask when she comes back? Dindet stared at the little toy, just wait. *Just wait…. Okay, no more waiting.*

Quickly, she slid off the stool and bounced toward the toy, scooping the dusty little contraption up to inspect in all its curious glory.

It was a hollow metal box shaped like a hexagon with a pointed lid and some little metal butterfly that stuck out the side.

Dindet tossed it in her hands for a moment, in meager attempt to figure out its function. She'd never dare touch a thing in the hateful house, but this place was warm and soft and tasted like sweet cream. So it felt more safe to do so.

The alien peered around for a moment in search of the wrinkly lady, catching a whiff of her warmth that led toward a small ajar door near the back door of the shop, and quietly made her way toward her.

The woman was doing something with another human toy that she spoke into, a phone if she recalled it correctly, but this one wasn't thin and made of glass with pictures on it. Instead, it was large and clunky, with a spiraled chord that connected to an even larger, clunkier thing with numbers and buttons on it.

Dindet sidestepped into the room and quietly stood behind the shop owner, more intent on getting her toy open than listening to the garbled nonsense she murmured into the phone-but-not-really.

"Yes, I have a lost little girl, dressed like a clown, I'm sure she is foreign? Perhaps you have a vacationing family at the ski lodge that misplaced her?" The woman spoke with a calm but quiet tone, unaware that the child behind her was not a child, and unaware that it was even behind her. Until a finger lightly tapped her shoulder, causing her to turn.

"Oh, you found something you like?" she said in a whisper while moving the not-phone under her other cheek. "It's a music box, darling, turn the key."

The elderly woman pointed at the metal butterfly, making a motion that imitated twisting, prompting Dindet to copy.

The clown turned over the box and twisted the key, cranking it as far as it could go until she let it go and some twinkling little noise softly came from the aluminum toy, repeating the same notes over in a mesmerizing little tune. And every time the melody ended an audible tick noise went off and the top of the box sprung open to reveal a very ratty-looking bear.

She nodded, and turned heel, moving back to the place the old lady told her to stay for the remainder of the day.

"There you are!" It was one of the familiar voices, the tall man. He caught her attention, staring at her with relief in his eyes but he tasted like salt and heat the moment she noticed him.

That wasn't nearly as vile as the taste the other one had though.

"Mrs. Deauxtree, I'm so sorry about this," Jon exclaimed, striding in with his arms outstretched, one that wrapped around Dindet's, pulling her off the stool and the other that went for a generous handshake with the elderly woman she now understood was a Doh-tree. "We only recently started the exchange program and I wasn't expecting her to go exploring on her own."

"Oh, Jon it's really fine, I thought she was a foreign tourist's daughter- if I had known she was with you, I would have sent Douglass and Theo to take her home. They've already left for the day though." The shopkeeper smiled softly, nodding back at Dindet, who managed to still hold the little music box. "You can take that with you if you like."

"Oh, no, we couldn't-"

"Nonsense, she's been listening to it all day, and I have plenty more music boxes. One off the shelf is nothing." Deauxtree interjected, reassuring the clown with a nod. "It's a little circus tune and she looks like she has a passion for that sort of thing."

"Right," Jon replied quietly, loosening his grip just slightly on the alien's arm. "Well, thank you so much for keeping an eye on her. We'll get out of your hair so you can close up."

***

Dindet sat in a metal box, much like the one she tinkered with in her hands, but this one had wheels and she was sure that this was what Oliver referred to as a car.

He sat next to her, seething with a boiling loathing that she could recognize in a heartbeat from just the few moments she had been around him. Every now and again, he would shoot a glare at her that she flagrantly ignored, focusing intently on the toy in her hands and not the horrid taste in her mouth.

"You can't just run off like that," He muttered, the disdain in his voice almost tangible. The clown didn't look up or even acknowledge him. "You really screwed up."

He knew his words were essentially lost on her, but the way she didn't even react, aside from turning over that stupid toy she got from Deauxtree was close to, if not, utterly infuriating.

Without thinking, Oliver ripped the box from her hands and tucked it beside him, out of her reach, finally then, did she look up.

There was a dumb, almost vacant stare on her face, aside from the way her paint swirled under her eyes in streaks down her cheeks.

The clown reached around him and effortlessly plucked the toy back, and as her focus returned to that, the paint returned to its regular, flower-like pattern.

"No," Oliver retorted, pulling the music box away once more. This time, Dindet shot a glare at him. "You don't deserve it, because you weren't supposed to leave."

The clown's eyes bore into him, but he held his stance. That is until the bright colors of her clothes began to turn dark crimson alongside the transitioning black marks around her eyes.

She pressed a single hand down on his chest, nearly digging newly formed claws into his skin while she silently took the toy back, warranting absolutely no further retaliation.

It may have been subdued, but Oliver recognized the sheer anger in her eyes, and that didn't even account for the not-so-subtle transformation. But he had seen her in a far more terrifying state, so was sure not to press any further.

The car pulled to a stop in the driveway of the cabin, and Jon was the first to exit, opening the door for the guest and his son to slide out.

"In the house, now. Please." His voice was stern, despite following it up with a mere pleasantry. Oliver shot one last glare at the clown before heading inside. And she, back to her usual hue, followed quietly behind him.

Foreign Exchange Student

He knew what was coming, and knew that the clown was in as much trouble as she was a guest. Still, there was a very slight, possibly minuscule amount of comradery between them under the gaze of his father.

Jon tapped his fingers on the kitchen island one by one, still contemplating what he should say.

"We have to come up with a plan," he stated, allowing Oliver to let out the breath of relief he had pent up from the tension.

"I just told Deauxtree, that it– um, Dindet, is a foreign exchange student.." He followed, waiting for at least one of them to catch up to the issue.

"Why is that a problem?" Oliver questioned, prompting a look of mild bafflement from his father.

"Her granddaughter's in your class, Theo Deauxtree? And her daughter works at the school too... she also mentioned Douglass being there." It took a moment, but it eventually dawned on him that the girl that tried to talk to him at the start of class was in fact,

Theophania Deauxtree. And Douglass mentioned secretly working for the antique shop.

"Wait- that's not fair! I can't bring her to school!" Oliver was quick to shoot down the idea, it would be a neverending nightmare if that stupid alien went to class with him. All because a dumb, mute clown would be constantly hanging around him like a personal children's birthday entertainer!

"I'm sorry, I kind of backed us into a corner, Ols. But I think I have a way to work around it." His dad casually grabbed a bowl from the cupboard and began making himself some cheap microwave curry. "You know those old clothes you forgot to donate?"

Oh no.

"Dad."

"I think they would fit her, right?"

This is a terrible idea. This is the worst idea ever. And somehow it came from the brain of a highly accredited scientist?

"Dad, it's not going to work." Oliver's voice nearly cracked at the thought, but his father persisted.

"No, no, look, I think- if we dress her up in your old clothes and teach her a few more words she can really pass as a foreign kid!" He smiled as if the thought was genuinely foolproof. "Then, we enroll her in class– some remedial English lessons, then she can actually communicate properly!"

"Whatever happened to 'if she spikes the radars we're dead'?!" Oliver shot a glare at Dindet, who seemed to have no idea or want to know what fresh hell he was about to go through.

"Well, I think I can come up with a harmless virus that shuts that down– I'd have to call Chris for a favor. It'll be fine! Win-win, you think?"

No. No! It's not a win-win, the only one winning here is you. My life is going down the gutter!

"What if she runs off again? What then?" he retorted, hoping that the argument was sound enough. His father almost laughed at the insinuation.

"It's gonna be fine Oliver, I promise."

Like hell it is!

Begrudgingly, reluctantly and every word in between, Oliver toted the witless clown up to his room to delve into the least favorite part of his closet.

"You better be grateful." He grumbled as he pulled open the closet door. Dindet stood behind him, watching him pull out box after box from the tiny room inside his larger, also room.

It was slightly more interesting than the music box, and she had learned a few new words that she was keen to practice. Even if he hated her, she knew Oliver was a word person.

"Alright, here you go." The boy pushed the boxes along the floor toward her and gestured for her to look inside them.

Now is the time, she thought, that was best to try the new word she learned, but be careful not to be so loud.

"What?" she questioned, pulling out a piece of fabric that was much longer than she initially anticipated. Oliver stared at it and his eyes quickly fell to the floor in abject embarrassment.

"It's a bunch of my old clothes," he answered bitterly, refusing to look at the dress. "Look, you're smaller than me and I only have this stuff cause I forgot to donate it over the summer. And I'm pretty sure you're a girl, so just take them."

Dindet hesitated, taking another look at the fabric, it was pink and blue and had little white flowers on it. Her eyes flickered back toward Oliver who looked keenly uncomfortable by the thing.

"Look, you gotta wear something other than...*that*." He gestured toward her vaguely, causing her to look down at herself. "Everyone is going to make fun of you if you look like that."

This endeavor was proving to be simultaneously unbearable, and a waste of time.

"Please just take them?"

Dindet blinked in confusion, honestly caught off guard by the taste of his discomfort. She lifted the garment and inspected it closely, trying to wrap her mind around its purpose.

"It's a dress." Oliver snapped impatiently, making her look back at him.

"Dress?"

"Yeah, you know, like what you wear? Girly clothes, skirts and tights, and stuff," he reiterated, almost flabbergasted by her innate inability to comprehend almost anything.

Dindet cocked her head slightly and began playing with the clothes as if it were something that it wasn't.

Dress was a new word and an entirely new concept to her, and she wasn't exactly aware of how she could articulate that. Not without diving into Oliver's loathsome thoughts.

"You are literally wearing a dress right now," he sighed as he brushed his fingers through his hair. "You do know that..right?"

Dindet's unperturbed face turned upwards in what looked like a mock expression of disgust.

"I am not." She objected, prompting an even heavier sigh from Oliver.

"Then what is all that?!" he exclaimed, gesturing at the bright orange petaled skirt, frilled collar, inexplicable bowtie combined with a gaudy green– tank top? Or sweater– he honestly couldn't tell where she stopped and the outfit started.

The clown briefly looked at herself as though she had never once thought about her outlandish appearance, then shrugged her shoulders.

"So..so you're–" He could feel his face burning at the childish idea. *Of course– I mean, come on, be the bigger person, Oliver.*

"What's a girl?"

What is with this freak?! What kind of question is that?

He almost couldn't stand it, and on some level, he wanted to believe she was playing a sick trick on him.

"You know, girls wear stuff like that, and uh–" he stopped himself from the gesture he was about to haphazardly commit to.

"They like to wear makeup sometimes, and–"

"I am not that." She cut in with deliberate affirmation. Once again, catching him completely off guard.

"Alright then!" He laughed through his yell, "*what* are you?"

Dindet cocked her head in a brief moment of thought before answering as matter of factly as possible.

"I am a clown."

"Aren't we all." Oliver breathed, too exhausted from the entire exchange to question any further.

Standing up, he kicked the other boxes toward Dindet and let out a disgruntled sigh. "These are yours now, I'm going to bed."

He began turning on his night lamp and the bathroom light to prepare for his much-desired nightly rituals, only to look back and notice that Dindet still sat on the floor digging through the boxes of clothes.

"I'm going to bed, that means you need to leave," he repeated in annoyance. This time, the clown stood up and focused whatever tiny attention span she had on him.

"Get out of my room." He stepped around the boxes and began shoving the alien toward his door until he reached the threshold and quickly shut it behind her, finally secure and alone in his room.

Sweet relief.

Oliver spun around and made his way back toward the bathroom, almost tripping on the boxes she had left on his floor.

He swiftly began turning on the shower water and changing out of the day's clothes.

All of this effort. Dad really, truly thinks that this dumb alien thing could help them bring Mom back. It's ludicrous.

Still though...one more day would be nice.

They would go to the nature park and take dangerous pictures of bears. Mom was weird like that. Then go to Mary Jane's for ice cream and eat it at the old courthouse gazebo. Mom would question one of Dad's articles with philosophy or some crazy physics theory and it would go right over both of their heads and it would be so funny because he would retaliate by shoving his ice cream on her nose.

We would all be happy doing the things we did on the weekends. Go home, Dad would stay up to do research, Mom would sit on the porch looking at the stars and when I can't sleep I would look down and see her petting Pancake...I'd make hot cocoa for the both of us just the way she likes it and go sit with her... she would tell funny stories about worlds that are exactly the same as this one but also just a little different.

That would be the one more day. It would be so nice. It would be—

"Oliver."

Oliver... Oliver?

Whatever moment of pleasant silence in the house was broken by a shrill screech that erupted from Oliver Tarsul's bedroom, followed immediately by the boy dragging a very confused Dindet down the stairs in his towel and throwing her onto the couch.

"You can't be in my room and you CANNOT be in my *SHOWER*!" He snapped, snatching up the television remote and flipping to something to entertain the bane of his existence.

"Sit here." Oliver softened his voice slightly. "And watch T.V. *Don't* get up from this spot, okay? And please, *please* stay out of my room?"

He hesitantly backed away from the clown, making sure to keep as much of an eye on her as possible, taking note of how quickly she became engrossed in old cartoons. He prayed that she would stay that way for as long as physically possible, before clambering back up the stairs to finish his shower.

***

Six A.M. the sun hadn't risen yet, and theoretically, neither should Oliver. Society and his stupid alarm clock dictated otherwise though, and so did his grades.

The boy turned over on his side with a groan, reluctant to escape the increasing comfort of his bed. Sadly, the alarm clock was more annoying, so he whipped one lackadaisical arm out and slammed it down on the off button, providing that sweet silence he longed for.

Slowly, he slid out from under the covers and plopped down on the floor in a dopey, sleep-deprived daze. A few moments of blinking, and rubbing the last bit of sleep from his eyes and he meandered toward the closet for a change of clothes.

The night was rough enough as it was, the day before even worse, but some part of him sincerely chalked it up to a wicked dream.

Until he caught sight of the light of the television and the unmistakable pronged jester hat that single-handedly ruined his life.

Dindet sat on the couch completely still, entirely mesmerized by the remnant of the adult shows that played right before the morning children's shows. If she heard him come down the stairs, she didn't seem to care.

She seriously sat there the whole night watching TV? Isn't she tired?

"Uh..good morning?" Oliver waved tiredly, garnering the clown's attention and her head swiveled around to face him.

"Good morning!" she repeated eagerly, climbing over the back of the couch to

reach him. "I know so many more words now!"

Fantastic. Now she's never going to shut up.

"That's great," he remarked, hoping his sarcasm reached her on some level.

"I know! Now I can be a person like you!"

Clearly not.

"How fun," he answered, walking past the bouncing thing to pour a bowl of cereal. "Are you gonna change or.."

"Oh, oh, look at this!" Dindet straightened herself slightly and began to change color, turning into that same oozing black, viscous material before completely returning to normal again, well, almost normal.

Somehow, she had managed to perfectly replicate the dress Oliver had given her, and mostly look like a person. The hat stayed though, which he was quick to point out.

"We can't wear hats in school." He reached toward the yellow dangling puff on one end, only for the clown to lean out of his range.

"No," she retorted sternly, grabbing the morphing moodring-esque accessory.

"Alright, suit yourself, but Principal Balboa is going to chew you out for it." Oliver shrugged.

"Morning, Ols." The not nearly as awake Jon yawned from the upper balcony of the hall, stumbling haphazardly down the stairs in fluffy pink slippers and traces of ink from the freshly mapped blueprints he had accidentally drooled on, marking his face like the morning after a nerds frat party. "G- ahhh...good morning, clown."

Jon frumped around the kitchen island in lackadaisical search of his much-desired coffee pot, murmuring quiet nothings to himself that neither Oliver nor Dindet quite understood before downing a cold, at least day-old brew.

"Eight," he said quietly, prompting confusion from his son.

"What's eight?" Oliver questioned through a mouthful of cereal.

"Eight security breaches," Jon replied with a yawn.

"I've got to complete at least eight government security breaches to pass her-" he gestured toward the clown with his mug. "Off as an exchange student from some country I haven't decided on yet."

"Oh," Oliver replied, shooting a slight glare at the alien.

"Oh- and I need a picture." Jon pulled out his phone, taking a quick snapshot of a very unprepared Dindet before slinking tiredly back to his makeshift attic lab. "I'll meet you guys at the admin office, just.. lemme take a little nap first."

Oliver shot another glare toward the clown that went presumably unnoticed.

It's her fault that they had to cover for her, and now dad's already had to clean up her stupid mess.

He quickly finished off the last of his cereal with an unceremonious gulp of the last bit of milk and made his way toward the doorway to the back porch to feed the cats.

"What are you doing?" Dindet asked, hoping that perhaps her new knowledge would garner a little more than the contempt Oliver seemed to have consistently on standby for her.

"Feeding the cats," he responded, already beginning to dread the rest of the day. *This was the best it was going to get with her around, wasn't it?* He really didn't want to imagine how the rest of the day was gonna go.

Oliver poured each bowl of food as a swarm of cats sauntered up from the outskirts of the forest. Each mewling for their portion before studiously turning an almost quizzical glance toward the new being in their vicinity.

Bacon was the first to snatch up his meal, taking advantageous opportunity over the others' curiosity toward Dindet, who lifted her feet awkwardly in gentle attempt to understand their interest.

It was infuriating. *They were obviously only interested because she was new and they never had guests over— they did the same thing the first time Douglass came over too.*

Oliver quickly pushed past her on his way up the road.

Dindet followed behind him quietly, stopping every now and then to look at something or other that caught her attention and catching up via some teleportation shenanigans he didn't understand nor want to.

He caught sight of the familiar semi-hunched stride of Douglass as the kid stumbled out of his house to greet him, taking a poignant moment of hesitation when he caught sight of the clashy-dressed stranger that bobbed and weaved behind Oliver like a lost puppy.

"Who's your friend?" he asked in lieu of a regular good morning. Oliver simply shrugged and sped up his pace, prompting Douglass to follow behind.

"Is she new?" Douglass spoke slightly quieter as to not garner Dindet's attention, he needn't worry though, as she was fairly preoccupied by the concept of bugs at the moment. "Is she the person you saw-"

"Dad signed up for the exchange program." Oliver cut him off with a short reply.

Douglass glanced back at the clown with slightly more intrigue.
"So that's why she looks so weird? Is- is that your–"
"Don't."

Oliver didn't look up when he spoke or answer loudly, but Dindet could taste his dread and slowed her pace just slightly, accidentally making eye contact with the other, slightly taller human with much curlier hair. It was the same one at the Doh-tree place.

Douglass straightened up and smiled at her, providing a welcoming wave of simple kindness.

"Hi, I'm Douglass, do you speak English?" The boy nearly yelled at her, adding to her mountain of quiet confusion. Dindet opened her mouth, hesitant to answer.

"I said, DO YOU SPEAK ENGLISH?" he repeated even louder. Oliver spun around and shot daggers at her.

"She's not deaf, Douglass," he replied, irritably gesturing toward her with a dismissive wave. "Just stupid."

"Say hi, Dindet," he commanded in disgruntlement. If she

weren't so annoying, and she didn't take everything so literally, and she wasn't such a freak...then maybe it would have been funny to him.

Dindet's eyes flickered from Oliver and back toward the other boy while she tried to understand.

"Hello, my name is Dindet."

Douglass smiled warmly at her and slowed his pace just enough that he walked only slightly ahead of her, taking some keen interest for a reason she didn't quite get. So far, aside from the yelling, he tasted much nicer than Oliver and almost as nice as the wrinkly old lady.

The three of them came to a halt at the edge of the dirt road connecting to the nicely paved backroad that the bus came down.

"Welcome to Pineton, it's pretty nice here," Douglass said.

***

Oliver was doing well enough. He took advantage of Douglass's monologuing nature and suggested he sit with the freak on the bus, hopefully talking her ear off about nothing and everything all at once.

"If you ever want to hang out or, I don't know, study, I live right down the road– I mean, you know that! We just walked to the bus stop, hah, sorry...I'll, I'll see you around, uh...Dindet?" Douglass blushed brightly as he stumbled down the steps, fumbling with his backpack awkwardly before ducking out of the way to let the confused clown out.

Oliver followed behind, grunting quietly to himself about how much a fool the poor kid was making of himself.

"Oh good, you're here!" Jon breathed in relief, seeing the two of them enter the office finally. He knelt down to share the situation.

"I managed to pull some strings," he said softly, "Dindet's officially a member of a reclusive northern European people here on a Visa and we are the family she's staying with, poor disguise aside, most people are just gonna think it's a culture thing. Lay low, don't cause any trouble, got it?"

"Dr. Jariwala, I have the files ready, now we just need to issue a student ID." Mrs. Deauxtree stepped through the back room of the office and toward a poorly maintained drape that would act as the backdrop to a school photo.

"And you must be miss Dindet? Just stand right here and smile while I take your picture. The ID should be done by the end of the day." The woman smiled and pointed toward the curtain and patiently waited for the clown to oblige.

"Perfect." She grinned after the flash went off. "Since she's only a little late to the year, we figured it would be easier to add her to Oliver's homeroom—"

What?

Whatever words came out of Mrs. Deauxtree's mouth next were entirely lost in the miniature, world-ending existential crisis that spun around Oliver's head and made it incredibly hard to focus. He blinked, trying to gather his thoughts before inadvertently getting himself detention through the sheer need to say some very, very undesirable things.

"I'm sure you'll be happy to show her around, won't you Ols?"

"Yeah...sounds great."

My entire world is coming to an end and I haven't even reached second puberty. All because of a stupid freaking clown.

It was said and done though. No amount of blissful wish-fulfillment, that the whims of the school would tear the parasite away. No, now he was more or less forced into being the leash hauler for something he never wanted in the first place. *It's fine. This is fine.*

Oliver nodded deafly at whatever the woman said- something about showing the clown around the school since she was new, though his thoughts were mostly filled with nonsense and an ear-piercing scream that he somehow put on repeat.

A hand clasped itself around his and squeezed lightly and for a moment, behind all the screaming, he heard a very quiet 'thank you', snapping him back from his existential meltdown.

He glanced down at the hand that held his, then slowly trailed his gaze upward toward Dindet's empathetic eyes which twitched with a slight wince when she offered a smile.

Lost kid.

No! No, no, no-no. Oliver pulled his hand free with a small disgusted 'blegh' and took a relatively large step away from the clown.

"Come on." He grumbled quietly, waving her forward to follow him as he led her around the school.

Dindet folded her hands together behind her back while she quietly meandered behind the boy, doing what she could to not dwell on the searing heat of his thoughts. It was hard enough not to chameleon into a beast around him, what with all his sincere loathing, but as horrible as it tasted it was sustenance nonetheless.

She imagined him as hot, painful, and almost unpalatable but not so bitter that it was unbearable. Sometimes it was, sometimes it was almost cool. And then there was this emptiness, at the center of everything else, blackening every other feeling that radiated off of him.

He also seemed to think about the familiar woman in the picture a lot.

"Auditorium, office, lunchroom, courtyard, atrium, gym." He rambled through names of the things he pointed to with abject boredom while the two toured the no longer bustling hallways filled with tiny and also much larger doors- only some of which led to places.

He stopped at one of the larger doors that read 'Mrs. Hargreaves' in colorful paper letters tackied to the wood.

"This is homeroom," Oliver mentioned, "English. And I'm in all AP classes."

There was a slight smirk in his voice as he spoke, knowing that the clown knew nothing of the suffering inside.

Dindet halted just behind him at the doorway and the floor felt like it had moved on without her.

Something is wrong here.

For a moment, an incredibly short one, Oliver caught a glimpse of fear streak across her stilled face.

Taking advantage of the opportunity, he stepped aside and swung open the door in an extravagant and gentlemanly display- if only to put that little horror on display for the rest of the class.

Dindet's head slowly leveled and her eyes focused onto the faces of several other human beings that all simultaneously turned to stare back at her.

She snapped a quick glance back at Oliver before he egged her on, providing a sickeningly sweet smile.

Then she stepped forward.

New Kid

indet looked out into the small sea of faces whose eyes all stared at her with contempt, confusion, and general nonchalance. And all she could do was simply stand there, quietly stalling out while her mind rapid fired out ideas to fill the silence.

"Class this is our new exchange student Dindet? Dindet." Another voice filled the silence for her, though she didn't move to see the owner.

"Please be respectful. Oliver, why don't you show her to her desk?" Mrs. Hargreaves gestured from the boy toward one of the empty desks along the last column.

He held back the little snicker at Dindet's complete lack of awareness, or perhaps sudden forced awareness, and casually strode into the room. He tugged her by the arm while she stared at everyone with her doe-eyed, dumb expression.

"Sit here." He directed, pointing at the seat behind and somewhat adjacent to his, far enough away but close enough that he could keep an eye— just in case she did something stupid, of course.

It was also directly next to Douglass's seat, and he wasn't one to pass up that opportunity.

Dindet followed Oliver's direction and sat down in the weird table chair combination, trying very, very hard to remain as still as possible to maintain some semblance of camouflage among these creatures.

Most of them had stopped staring at her now, and the tall woman whose name was taped to the door began talking about Poes and amontillados.

"Psst." Someone hissed quietly, prodding her in the arm to grab her attention. Dindet swiveled her head to search for them, catching sight of a- what she presumed to be 'girl' smiling at her.

"My name's Cassidy! Tambedou, it's so cool to have another first-gen here!" Cassidy gave a big grin to the clown. Completely unaware that Dindet was still in the process of determining the difference between the arbitrary concept of girls, whatever Douglass and Oliver were, and what kind of human a Doh-tree was. So she just stared at her.

This Cassidy had long and thick chunks of coils for hair with little aluminum rings to decorate them, and big circular metal rings with glass inside them perched on her nose. The girl tasted warm and sweet and rich, which was refreshing compared to the dull flavor of boredom around her.

"You need a book," Cassidy said in a low whisper, nodding toward a shelf with several of the exact same book piled on the bottom rung. "If you want, we can share."

The girl pushed her open book toward Dindet, allowing her to take it and peer down at the amalgamation of letters that she knew formed words.

Words that she mostly could also understand, but they had a lot more letters than she realized, which made parsing them out in her head far more complicated than need be.

So instead, she simply stared at the page full of letters and decidedly didn't even try.

She would work on that later.

Besides, Oliver didn't seem to care all that much because he had his head buried into a notebook that he scribbled in instead of the book that he was supposed to be interested in.

***

He didn't particularly care for the macabre topic that the school year decided to start on. Poe already wasn't his favorite, but on some level, he figured it was a result of the collective shellshock that finished out the end of the year prior.

Upperclassmen always rumored the halls that Mrs. Hargreaves liked to switch around the syllabus to suit the mood. Apparently, death and pestilence were the moods for the start of the year.

As opposed to taking part in the class reading of The Cask of Amontillado, he decided his time was better spent doodling. It kept his mind off of fresh death and the reason that sat just behind him.

Though, when his meandering thoughts returned to the clown he dug his pencil into the paper, resulting in several broken pieces of lead.

"Okay, for the last thirty minutes I want you to discuss the previous passage with your peers and create groups of four." The teacher lightly tapped the whiteboard and pulled up the projector screen to reveal what could quite possibly be the absolute worst thing to start the year with.

A group project.

"Each group is going to pick a paragraph from the short story and present an analysis of that paragraph, and how it relates to you in current day. It's due in two weeks so please choose wisely."

He could already feel the piercing gaze of Dindet on his back, knowing full well that this was going to be even more of a nightmare than he initially hoped. *But when has anything ever been easy, right?*

"Yes, we can-"

"Do you want to be in my group?" Another person cut him off mid-sentence, pulling the clown's attention away from him and toward Cassidy, the girl who sat next to Dindet on her other side.

"Douglass and I were gonna team up and we figured you might want to be with people close by." The girl offered before any objection by Oliver could be made. Dindet's eyes flickered from Cassidy to Oliver and back in silent hesitation.

"Okay."

Okay?

What like I haven't been holding your hand through— it doesn't matter.

"You can be in our group too, if you want." Douglass piped up, directing the comment at Oliver.

"Yeah, sure." *The better option, since I am sort of obligated to keep an eye on her.*

"Perfect!" Cassidy grinned, pulling out a neatly kept notebook with several colorful tabs. "We can divvy up everyone's duty so we each have something to do."

"That way we all do something and get credit for the whole thing. Plus, sorry, but I have the best handwriting out of all of us," Cassidy remarked, closing the notebook and stuffing it into her bag.

Quietly, and as inconspicuous as possible, Dindet fretted over the entire concept, shooting a very nervous glance toward Oliver, who looked to be dealing with his own thoughts.

Shortly after that, the bell rang and all the other kids stood up and began meandering toward their prospective friend groups, chatting and musing about things she didn't really care about aside from this new challenge placed in front of her for no comprehensive reason.

Another presumed 'girl' made her way toward their corner of the room and began talking to Oliver, who flagrantly ignored her.

"Is she why you ditched school yesterday?" she asked, throwing a sideways glance toward Dindet.

Oliver buried his head further into his arms in an effort to ignore the girl, much to no avail as she promptly smacked her hand on the table, causing him to jump and raise his head with a meaningful glower.

"Why does it matter?" he mumbled, bowing his head once more.

Dindet watched as the girl began to turn more pink, tasting something like cinnamon pepper and sugar when she stared down at him in search of an answer.

"Because I was gonna tell you something yesterday," she answered, a little too loudly.

Oliver peeked out from behind his arms once more. "So? Just tell me now?"

At this, the girl became even more flustered, shuffling from foot to foot.

"It doesn't matter anymore- God." She shot another quick glare at Dindet, who by now was watching the entire interaction fairly intently. "Stop eavesdropping, freak!"

"Theo, don't be mean." Cassidy bit back in Dindet's defense.

"ThEo DoN't Be MeAn. Alright, mom." The girl, Theo, mocked while she walked back to her desk.

Students that had been standing began filing back to their seats as an inordinately skinny man stumbled into the classroom with a laptop case in hand.

"Alright, class– oh, a new kid!" He interrupted himself mid-sentence upon sight of Dindet's unorthodox fashion sense. "Don't let Principal Balboa see you with that hat on."

The comment prompted the clown to lightly tug on the tress of her cap, still steadfast in not removing it.

"Anyway, welcome to a new year, last year was fun and I'm sure you all had a wonderful– mostly wonderful summer break..." the teacher paused, "but now you get to learn the fun stuff! Physics!"

There was an audible groan that resounded from the kids at the mere mention of the idea.

Another one?!

Dindet sunk back in her seat at the idea of this strange crucible of knowing things that she didn't know, and she dreaded the possibility of more reading.

"So, yesterday I was really easy on you guys with a simple equation–" the teacher began scribbling numbers and letters on the whiteboard, ignoring the sounds of exasperation from the students as the equation nearly doubled in size. "Today is gonna be a toughy, see if you can tell me what this is."

It wasn't long before nearly everyone was lost on the answer, which prompted the man to provide some semblance of encouragement.

"Come on guys, easy question. Does anyone know what it is? Anyone?" He scanned the room for hands, watching each and every student lower their heads and avert their eyes, all except the flashy colorful hat girl, who looked at the equation like it was a fresh meal.

"How about you– uhh.." He glanced down at the roll, finding a little sticky note with what he hoped was her name. "Dindet? You know what this is?"

The clown jumped slightly in her seat as if struck from the mathematical trance she inadvertently placed herself in.

"It's um–" She hesitated, trying to find the right words to use. "You use it to find answers about elementary particle physics."

That was mostly right, the equation was complex and a nonlinear integral equation with two variables, and it would take a couple minutes for her to figure it out, but she was mostly there.

"It's supposed to mathematically describe clow- elementary particles. The, uhm, one of the smallest components of matter, I can solve it if you–"

"No, no, you don't actually have to solve it! I just wanted to know if you knew what it was!" The teacher laughed, brushing his fingers through his slicked hair in excitement. "H-how did you know that?"

Dindet blinked at the man, not quite understanding the question.

"I'm a-..n...exchange student?" Close one, thanks to Oliver's very quick jab into her side.

The teacher smiled widely and whipped around to write more underneath the equation.

"Well, Dindet you're very bright." He congratulated as he finished writing out in large letters, 'QUANTUM PHYSICS'.

"Since the year is just starting and likely none of you enjoy math at all, I decided to start off the syllabus with something a little more entertaining than your average velocity equation." The teacher clapped his marker down on the tray and began pointing at random students.

"Theo, do you know what aspects of quantum physics are used in the AKAN lab?"

The rude girl shrugged her shoulders and mumbled idle grievances into her sleeve.

"How about you?" The teacher pointed at Douglass, patiently waiting for an answer.

The boy shifted awkwardly in his seat before perking up with a decent reply.

"I know my Dad worked on the supercollider, so particle physics?" He offered, prompting a victorious little fist pump from the teacher as he turned to write it down.

He then spun around and pointed at Oliver, whose head was firmly buried in his arms.

"You, do you know what else they work on at the lab?"

Oliver tilted his head, mumbling inaudibly to himself before sitting up and heaving a discontent sigh.

"Nuclear physics, Astrophysics, Quantum physics, particle physics, chemistry, quantum mechanics, bionuclear mechanics, and the study of relative matter in dimensional space– which doesn't currently have a name in the scientific field yet." His answer was followed by the return of his head into his arms that he dearly hoped would lead to a nap.

"You are correct!"

"I know." Oliver breathed quietly.

"Do you know why the AKAN lab studies these subjects? Oliver, please sit up."

"They want to be at the forefront of discovering the existence of alternate parallel dimensions and potentially use them to travel long distances in space." This was the same diatribe that the tour guides would vomit up every other year when the AP physics class took a field trip to the lab. He had been there hundreds of times with his parents, and it was always, *always* the same.

"Correct again, Oliver, so you must know that this is the year our class goes on the lab field trip? Your parents also work there, don't they? I'm sure they both will have plenty to educate us on."

"Not anymore." Theo cut in, twisting in her seat to face Oliver. "You didn't hear? There was a big accident and his mom died."

Oliver stared at her, his eyes flickering around the room at all the other kids' faces that had turned his direction. *Why would she say something like that?*

"Theo," Cassidy began, "that's really not okay–"

"Why not?" Theo interrupted with a shrug, "you're not upset about it still, right?"

"Class," the teacher attempted to draw the students' attention back to him, though it went largely ignored.

She turned her gaze back to Oliver. "Now that you're totally loaded, you can pay for all your *surgeries*."

"I- I, I'm not–" He fumbled with his words, struggling under the pressure of being put on the spot so abruptly. "I don't actually–"

Kids began to murmur softly to one another, and every spare word Oliver caught mounted up inside him. *Of course. Of course, that would be the first rumor of the year.*

"Class." The teacher attempted.

Oliver shuddered and drew in on himself, unable to cease the increasingly loud chatter of the room as everyone talked so incessantly.

"My theory is that they were working on, like, some top-secret area 51 stuff and the whole thing got ganked," one kid said, nudging the classmate to his right.

"Oh no, see I bet she just drank some acid labeled wrong, you know?"

"Labeled wrong, or you think on purpose? They do some seriously crazy stuff there, my uncle said his friend used to be a janitor there. And *that guy* said they were a front for a cartel."

"Class, settle down."

"That's dumb," another student interjected, "Douglass just said they had a super collider, it probably broke and shoved us into some parallel dimension."

Dindet's head swiveled around in attempt to keep track of the erupting multiple conversations taking place. The room had gone from stark and white to a myriad of colors as each student spouted off their theories, building upon every one of them. All while Oliver sat in his chair, silently turning the room black as the vile flavor of his grief and discomfort whipped and lashed against every disjointed feeling that resided there amongst them.

"No, see, I know exactly what happened," Theo stated loudly, slamming her fist on her desk in order to get the students' attention. Oliver flinched, pressing his palms into his lap. *Shut up.*

"She obviously killed herself and made it look like a big accident." She began explaining her theory. "It's way too easy to think that they have aliens or whatever, but think about it, having a freak like Oliver for a kid?"

Shut up. Shut up. Shut UP

She turned to face him, "that's not even your real name, it's-"

"STOP TALKING!" Oliver bolted up and slammed his hands down on his desk, startling her from finishing. He trembled, glaring the girl down and forcing her to clamp her mouth shut with the hatred in his eyes.

The room had gone quiet, but he didn't care. All he wanted in that moment was to make that stupid girl know just how awful he felt.

She wouldn't do that. She was a good person, a good mom and she would never, ever do something like that. She wouldn't just leave knowing what would happen.

"Oliver." The teacher's voice pulled him from his white-hot anger and Oliver drew in a quick gasp when his hand rested on his shoulder. "Please step outside for a moment."

Oliver's demeanor shifted, and he pulled away from his seat, reluctantly and quietly following Mr. Chavez out the classroom door and to the hall.

They returned a few minutes later, Oliver went back to his seat, and Mr. Chavez continued class as if nothing at all had changed.

But the classroom atmosphere proved otherwise.

***

It took a few minutes for the static of tension in the room to die down. Mostly due to Dindet breaking through it with answer after answer for even the most complicated physics equations Mr.Chavez threw at them.

It would be a lie to say that Oliver and in turn nearly half the class were both flabbergasted and resentful of Dindet's mathematical aptitude.

Of course, he was the only one who knew it was inhumanly so, which shed a little more light on why his Dad needed her so badly. Understanding math and physics and chemistry came so effortlessly to her that it made him contemplate smacking his head against his desk on several occasions throughout the day.

It wasn't until after the day had ended he got that fantastic and recognizable superiority when she waited patiently for the entire class to leave.

The clown clapped her hands down his desk and let out a groan as she melted into the floor, changing color until she resembled some kind of half-baked Jackson Pollock.

"I can't read!" she exclaimed, followed by a weak whimper from under the desk. Oliver bent over in his seat to catch the ever-desired despair he longed for.

She was half of a puddle, the upper part of her torso wrapped around a leg of the desk while the other half bled out in an orangey-black pool on the floor.

He almost thought about taking a note of the colors she could turn to, but decidedly thought it better to simply enjoy this moment for what it was. He needed it.

"It's not my problem." He shrugged, getting up out of his seat and heading out without even waiting for her.

Granted, that didn't do anything because as soon as he lost sight, she appeared on the other side of the doorway, with a face that seemed to shift along with her Kaleidoscope of colors.

"But– but you helped me before?" she stammered, reaching for his arm before quickly pulling back in hesitation.

"Yeah, well, you haven't done anything for me, so why should I help you now?"

All but show off how stupidly smart she was.

He watched as her eyes darted from left to right in thought before she snapped into that usual look of hers with a smile.

"I can help with math?" She offered, popping in front of him from nowhere without even the notion of a thought if anyone noticed.

"That's what my Dad's for," Oliver remarked, walking just a little faster in effort to outpace her. The clown reappeared at the corner as he turned to follow him further, and for a moment, she looked out of breath.

"I can, uh, I can take you somewhere really cool?" Now that was an offer that piqued his interest.

It's not like he didn't notice she could teleport, odds were, she knew of some very interesting places. He contemplated the idea, ignoring her growing desperation in exchange for something else she might do for him.

"How about both? And– and you have to do one other thing for me," he bargained, slowing down just enough to see her think about it.

"What other thing?" she asked, dipping behind him to avoid the pillar she nearly walked through.

"I haven't decided yet, but when I do you gotta do it, okay?" He needed time to think about it, something good, truly heinous, hopefully, something that would make her stop bugging him all the time.

"I don't-"

"Do you want to read or not?" he threatened, spooking whatever doubts out of her right then and there. Dindet nodded. "Cool, then it's a deal."

***

Oliver trudged down the steps of the bus, followed by a much bouncier Dindet, and then by Douglass who looked just about like he were going to explode if caught more than two feet away from the clown and by extension, Oliver himself.

"It's pretty convenient that the three of us are close together, makes the project easier to work on– plus we got Cassidy's number so we can keep tabs on everyone's jobs," Douglass remarked, swaying to and fro between his other classmates to show off his new contact.

"And if you want, you can come over to my house to work on the poster."

He smiled at the two of them in hopes of gaining some kind of reply. Or at least one from the new girl– he knew Oliver wasn't much for talking as it was. Especially after Theo practically plowed over his nerves.

Dindet briefly glanced at him and offered a smile in return, which immediately made his face burn at the sight.

"So..is it normal to uh, uhm, look the way you do where you're from?" Definitely not the most tactful way to say that she objectively stood out from the crowd but what else could Douglass say? You look like a circus performer?

The girl's smile dropped and her eyes flitted toward Oliver as if she was expecting him to give permission before she answered.

"I think so?"

Not the best answer either, but Douglass was keen to be respectful, at least somewhat.

"So, everyone looks like a clown where you're from? Is– Is it like a circus colony?" The boy mentally smacked himself at the idea. *Circus colony? It could be like a sacred cultural ritual thing! Way to belittle it down to just a circus. You're literally the worst Douglass.*

He winced in anticipation, watching her mull over the idea with dread.

"Well, I haven't really met other clo– people..like me, not exactly the same at least." Dindet slowed her pace slightly so she could walk beside him as opposed to Oliver. "But there are definitely more than just me."

Okay, that's a decent answer, but something about it just felt..off.

"So it's like a culture thing?"

"Uh.." Dindet looked back at Oliver once more. "Yes?"

By this time he was keenly listening to their conversation, slowing just enough that he was only a few paces in front of them.

"Oh cool, so what are you?"

"Oh, I'm an in-"

"She's from northern Europe," Oliver interrupted, turning

heel to face them in a backward walk. "A secluded group from northern Europe."

His sudden input caused the two to face him, breaking off whatever conversation was had when Dindet half jogged to walk beside Oliver instead of Douglass, forcing the boy to part from them as they neared his house.

"Well, I guess I'll talk to you later?" Douglass said as he veered off toward his home with a mild wave farewell.

"Bye Douglass," Oliver half hollered back.

"Bye Dindet! Bye Ols!" Douglass answered, catching one last glimpse of his very much newfound crush as she swiveled around to wave back.

***

"Dad, I'm home!" Douglass called, shrugging off his backpack at the living room and immediately moving toward the blue glow of the garage doorway. "We got a new girl in class this year."

"You do?" Faint enough behind the whirring of a nondescript thing Douglass didn't care to understand, his dad answered back.

"Yeah, she's a foreign exchange student living with Oliver."
"Oliver?"

"Tarsul?" Douglass clarified as he rounded some large metal contraption with an inordinate amount of cables running to and from the thing.

"Oh, Jon's...son– have you noticed anything strange around their place as of recent?" He redirected, moving back toward a pile of oily and grimy tools to pick from.

"No, I mean, nothing super unusual– I know Dr. Jariwala is working on a project, cause I see the attic light on like, all the time." Douglass picked out the wrench his father had been looking for and handed it over so he could continue.

"Yes, yes, he sent me an email today about some of the security facilities at the lab and asked if I knew anything about radiation counters– I don't imagine what he's working on is too dangerous though," his father replied, digging back into the circuitry of his machine. "You mentioned a new girl at school?"

"Oh, yeah, her name is Dindet and she's from...uh, somewhere in Europe, she's really nice and pretty cool– she dresses kind of funny, but I think that just makes her cooler– unique, I guess," Douglass answered with much more enthusiasm, enough that his dad paused his work for a moment to knock him lightly in the gut with a dirty elbow.

"Seems like you're pretty taken with her?" He mocked with a smile, wrapping an arm around Douglass to bring him closer and help him with his work.

"You should invite her over, maybe you'll have yourself a little school time fling?" The notion brought some of the brightest of blushes to Douglass's face as his dad pulled away from him to move back to work on whatever thing it was he was working on.

"What's this supposed to be?" Douglass asked, stepping around the chords and coils and rather unsafe open wires that wrapped around grounds and bolts.

"Well, I've been keeping track of the star alignments for the past couple of months– haven't been able to sleep very well."

"And I noticed that all our constellations have moved about 45 degrees north, judging by the degree I figured the earth's axis is out of alignment, or the gravitational pull of the sun grew a few million tons in the past– I dunno, three days?" The scientist continued, "Which brings up the project Jon's working on and his odd request of me."

Douglass fiddled with some small metal remote-looking contraption as his father spoke, only really half-listening while he talked about probably anything but the actual subject he had asked about. At least, until his dad patted his shoulder to grab his attention.

"You know, he asked me if I had any intel from AKAN?" He quieted slightly, "I imagine it must have something to do with the incident earlier this year, it was Marie's lead project after all... poor man must be all kinds of lost right now."

There was a pause between them, almost like a miniature moment of silence before he perked up again and grabbed the device from his son's hands.

"Anyway, I'm working on an electromagnetic frequency disruptor, hopefully, I'll be able to configure it well enough to create a clean energy source and get some of my funding back," he finally answered with a smile.

Douglass's father tossed the small remote-looking toy in his hands for a moment of pride.

"This was the prototype, and this–" He smacked his hand down on the much bulkier, heavier machine. "Is the final product. It essentially combs through the air attracting electrodes and creates a contained tesla arc. Only issue I've run into is that the larger one requires a ridiculously high amount of electrodes to produce the energy needed to run the town."

The man tapped on the machine in a brief pause of thought.

"I think I can build a better current if I have something that conducts electricity well, maybe some biopsied electric eels from the lab.." He began to devolve into quiet murmurs of potential prospects.

"You can have the small one if you want, show it to that new friend of yours, impress her maybe."

Douglass glanced back at the smaller contraption that his dad set down on his desk, picking it up to inspect it a little closer.

It looked like an odd combination of a taser, remote control, and a very small, clunky television set. It was nice and compact though, and he doubted anyone would find it dangerous at school. *Maybe, I could pop by Oliver's this evening– or would that seem a little too eager?*

He was no fool at courting– he had seen every single Pride and Prejudice, even the extended cuts and just about every romantic comedy under the sun. An indispensable wealth of knowledge for the young man erring to venture forth into the teen dating scene. At least, that's what he imagined.

So, he decided to show him– her later, maybe tomorrow, maybe after the school project? He would of course have to come up with a plan.

Lesson Number One

"First off, don't tell anyone where you're from, or people will put two and two together," Oliver grumbled after Douglass departed, making sure they were far enough that he couldn't hear. "You're lucky he's about as smart as a box of rocks."

Dindet glanced back and offered a small wave to the boy as he called goodbye to them, not quite gathering the same level of severity Oliver seemed to feel about the situation.

"Is that a good thing?" she asked softly.

"Yeah, because if he were any smarter you would have totally blown our cover and ruined all my dad's work," he answered gruffly. "You're a liability."

"Is that-"

"It's not a good thing, it means you're dangerous." He kept walking, despite hearing her come to a halt, something deep inside him knew he hit a nerve, but he also was a little terrified to turn around– in case she turned into a monster again.

"I'm not.." It was probably the least convincing defiance he had ever heard, but there was a soft gasp in her voice, like someone who was choking back tears, and that was what forced his feet to stop.

She stood a good twenty feet back, and had turned a blotchy bluish-purple, her fists tightly balled and to her sides.

Her eyes were trained on the ground as her face seemed to animate something akin to tears trailing down her cheeks.

"A- I..I'm–" *What am I doing? Apologizing? I'm not the one who parades around the halls popping in and out of space and changing color and dressing like every day is Halloween!*

"It's not like I'm wrong though," he argued, taking long strides back to meet her. "You don't even care who sees you, I mean– you melted into a puddle in class and you change color, not to mention your face! It's a miracle you lasted the day at all. I don't get why you're upset– it's dumb. *You're* dumb, and I can't believe you actually think that people don't think it's suspicious at all. You're an alien and a freak and you don't even try to act or look like a person. *Obviously, you can!* If you can make your own clothes and change color and shapeshift and whatever– then you should be able to at least *LOOK* like a normal kid. But you *don't*."

Oliver huffed, finishing his tirade.

The alien raised her head slowly, her eyes widened and a small smile began to creep across her face as her colors returned to their gaudy normalcy.

Wait. That's not how the reaction should be.

No, she was definitely much cheerier, still a little blue– literally. But whatever cogs in her brain were turning up something that Oliver genuinely wanted nothing to do with, considering even the worst of his words apparently didn't affect her at all.

***

It was fine. She was sure now. He didn't actually mean it. Well, he did, and he was sort of right. She wasn't really trying to blend in, but was there really a need? No one seemed to care much. They were far more occupied by him.

She did a particularly good job ignoring the little black thought in the back of her mind that echoed the voice of something terrible. The one that grew ever so slightly larger as the seconds ticked by.

"Oh... I understand now." The vacant answer was really all that came to her mind. *Be nice. Be nice because this is all you have and you're safe. For now.*

Dindet closed her eyes in a forced little smile, happy colors, happy thoughts, and she stepped past him before blinking entirely out of his capable sight.

The places she liked to go most– where no one really looked, were always sideways to the place she was initially. Time was slow here, and she could spend hours, months, years milling around in the in-between of worlds and when she came back most humans would think she was gone a couple of seconds.

Now would be a good time to tear herself apart bit by bit in a horrendous attempt to fix something that she knew wasn't fixable. It was a nasty idea that would go nowhere.

However, it always remained, that soft, tender part of her that always reminded her that she was not supposed to *be.*

Dindet sat down on the back porch of Oliver's home, staring into the colorless sky and pretending very, very hard that she wasn't nearly as upset as she was. *It's okay.*

Maybe it's time to go back now.

Oliver was very slowly making his way through the house to feed the small furry things that were beginning to huddle around where Dindet was and was not. So she decided that if she stayed as still as possible, and held up all her body that it wouldn't show, and then later, she could do something to make him happier.

***

"Wow, it's like you never left." Oliver's voice dripped with sarcasm as he opened the back door. *Of course, she wouldn't run off.*

She should have.

He said awful things but she was more resilient than he

anticipated, and his insides turned at the thought of her actually leaving.

Maybe because she was sort of like his personal punching bag for all that pent-up rage and anxiety surrounding him at every turn.

But also probably because on a very small, secretive level, she refused to leave and that meant that she actually, maybe, possibly, enjoyed his company.

That made his stomach churn and twist into knots of the most unbecoming kind of guilt.

She hadn't answered him and was instead enamored with the cats that swarmed around her for cuddles and pets.

"Look..I–" He hesitated, taking a moment to shake the anxiety off. "I probably shouldn't have said that to you."

He waited, hoping for her to at least turn around, but she only lowered her head to smile down at Bacon.

It felt like a rock was lodged in his chest, but Oliver brushed his hands through his hair to calm his nerves just a little more.

Why is this so nerve-wracking?!

"I know you're probably scared, and...alone, and don't really know anything about where you are or what's going on..or know what to do..and..." He almost choked on the words as he spoke. "And, maybe want someone to help you figure it out. So..so I'm sorry I've been mean. It's just..a lot for me too."

"I understand."

It doesn't sound like it. It sounds like she wants me to go away. Like she was sad. I...messed up.

"I mean, you're not really that dumb, you're really good at math and shape-shifting is actually uh, really cool..what I mean is.. is that I don't hate you." Oliver fiddled with his thumbs, awkwardly trying to save face and maybe fish for forgiveness.

"Please don't lie to me."

What?

"W-what?" Oliver dropped his hands in confusion, the clown

finally turned to look at him. She scratched a finger on the porch boards thoughtfully before glancing up to provide some explanation.

"I know how you and Mr. Your Dad feel about me...I know how everyone feels– all the time." She answered calmly, breaking that line of sight to pet Pancake. "Hate is red and hot and not very nice to taste..but it's all I have right now."

Oliver averted his eyes, folding in on himself with guilt. *She could tell the entire time?*

He wasn't particularly subtle, but the shame of it crept over his shoulders and held him there, awkwardly standing in front of an alien he hated without reason and never with secret.

"I-it's okay though! I know it's a big jumbly mess of feelings– not just hate!" Dindet retracted lightly, climbing up to be a little closer to him. She hesitated for a moment, then pressed her hand into his shoulder. "It's okay to feel a lot of different things all at once."

Oliver stiffened, recognizing the words she spoke as something his mom said when he was upset. Even the warmth in her voice echoed hers. He dragged in an unsteady breath and nodded, quickly pulling out of Dindet's reach in effort to escape the overwhelming anguish that rose in his throat like bile.

"R-right.." He breathed. "let- let's work on the school project."

How did she know that? How did she know that would be exactly what mom would say?

***

Oliver glanced up every so often to look at the clown, inspecting and trying to find traces of anything that would give away that she knew what he felt.

I don't even know what I feel– how is she supposed to?

She didn't look any different, at least not in a way he could tell. She was lying on her stomach on his floor practicing writing a few really simple sentences he had made for her.

She had already finished his math and physics homework within about five minutes of starting it, so now all that was left was teaching her to read so she could actually comprehend the text paragraph they were supposed to present.

He watched her intently as she poked herself with the wrong end of the pencil in an attempt to mimic him when he took notes.

"Why are you so good at math and stuff? You know things that we don't even teach," he questioned from atop his bed, resting his chin on the pillow between his legs.

Dindet cocked her head to one side as she began to scribble illegibly on the paper.

"I have to, or else I can't go anywhere."

"You mean, like when you teleport?" he rephrased, scooting a little closer to check her work. It was horrendous but getting better. Slowly.

"I don't teleport. I just go somewhere else where time is slower and come back here, in the place I'm supposed to be. But faster," she clarified– if that could be considered clarification. To Oliver, it made less sense than teleporting.

"But you could just walk the same distance. It sounds like more effort than it's worth," he retorted quietly, only slightly jealous of the ability, mostly because it was a tad annoying that she could just go anywhere she wanted in a blink of an eye, and he couldn't.

"Yeah." Dindet sighed before twisting up to look at him and promptly reappearing on the bed next to him. "But it's faster in this dimension. I mean, if I really wanted I could teleport, but I don't know this place very well yet."

Oliver rolled over to the other side of his bed and reached to grab her practice sheets and hand them back to her with an incredulous look.

"But you're still doing the same work. Also, how are you able to shape-shift, and change color?" *It was kind of dumb to never ask but now was as good a time as any.*

Dindet plopped her head down on her hands with a thoughtful little hum.

"I'm made of matter? And I can control all of it. Even stuff that isn't me." She plucked the pencil out of Oliver's fingers and held it up to give an example. "See?"

The pencil vibrated profusely in her grasp until it turned into a liquidy substance that morphed and floated like a gelatinous bubble in the air. It condensed once more to form another pencil, but instead of yellow, it was now red.

"To change color all I had to do was change the way it refracted light. It works the same for me," she remarked, handing the pencil back to Oliver and deciding her time was better spent popping to the corner to look at little soapstone sculptures he'd made a year ago.

"Then why do you change color all the time?"

At that, Dindet seemingly shuddered, as though the notion made her deeply uncomfortable. But she quickly saved face with a placid smile.

"I only change color when I eat."

"Well." Oliver glanced up from his homework, quietly eyeing the way she practically evaded the true intent of his question. "What do you eat?"

"Feelings."

He sat up and set his papers down, watching the alien as she became increasingly more uncomfortable with the topic. She flickered through a kaleidoscope of colors and they all began to bleed together until all at once she grew unnaturally stiff.

"What was that thing you got so mad about?" Dindet twisted around, turning her discomfort right back onto him. "At school today? You tasted the same about the thing I saw."

Oliver grumbled and muttered small nothings until he finally answered, once again, "it's not your problem."

An Afternoon Romp

"**S**o, if you can go to a place where time slows down– does that mean you can time travel too?" Oliver shot a quick glance at the photo on his nightstand, opting to switch the subject to something slightly more palatable.

"Well..yes, and no? I think?" Dindet's vague answer didn't really sate the real question nagging at his mind.

"So you can't go back into the past to– I dunno...talk to someone? Or try to get them back– or, or figure out why you came here for real?" The boy shifted in his seat in an effort to hide that little yearning in his heart.

Dindet followed his gaze, tasting an undeniable sickness that made her almost want to retch. Her eyes flickered back to the kid and she caught some inkling of the source. A terribly black hole that seemed to open up in the center of him and suck every pure thought deep into its abyss.

"No..." she mumbled, a little too distractedly, "it's more like..well– I could just show you? If you want?"

The offer caught Oliver's attention and he sat upright to face her. "What do you mean?"

"Well." Dindet pressed a finger to her cheek in contemplation, coming up with some sort of solution. "I know this place that is really good for explaining it– and it's also really fun. And, I promised to take you somewhere cool, remember?"

She lowered her head briefly. "I've never taken anyone anywhere before though, so hopefully it will be okay..."

She spoke softly, mostly to herself it seemed. "I could probably unmake you..and then move you, and remake you and if it works out, you won't turn into mush."

"Mush?" Oliver glanced down at himself, starting to get a little less interested and a little more worried about the idea of traveling through dimensions.

"Well...if I don't do that, then I might accidentally explode you. And I wouldn't be able to remake you because I probably don't know all your properties– and I'd feel really bad about it," Dindet explained, still mulling over the different ways she could potentially deconstruct an entire living human being, move them, and reconstruct them without killing them. It wasn't exactly an easy task, and it wasn't the least consuming either.

"I think I can do it," she finally answered, grabbing the boy's hand and pulling him off the bed.

"Wait– what about mush?!" Oliver retorted, more than wary of the consequences if she failed. Dindet offered a sly little grin and tugged a little harder.

"Don't worry, I'm 65% sure it'll be fine!"

"What about the other 45?!" He clenched his eyes shut and pulled hard, breaking free from the clown's iron grip and stumbling backward a couple of feet.

"See? I told you it would be fine." Dindet clasped her hands behind her back and rocked on her feet in subtle triumph. "You can open your eyes now."

Oliver winced in anticipation before opening one eye, then the other.

Just about every aspect of everything around him had completely been replaced by an entirely different world.

His room, the house, all of Pineton was replaced by rolling hills made of something like fleece quilts patched together with giant threads. Mountains made of decorated pillows and bushes made of balls of yarn.

The sky was a teal blue and cotton balls hung in the sky as clouds covered in childish glitter.

It was a kindergarten craft fever dream and unbenounced to Oliver, the entire time he was enthralled by this new real and unrealistic location, Dindet had successfully wrapped him up in at least five hundred feet of thick red yarn, to the point he resembled a cherry with his head as a stem.

"I figured you might like this place, just watch out for the giant babies," she casually remarked, pulling his attention back to her.

"Giant what?"

Instead of providing an explanation, Dindet held up a finger and booped the boy on the nose, perfectly so that the weight of his swath tumbled him backward down the hill screaming.

Panicked shrieking quickly turned into a nervous howl of amusement. He unraveled out of the throngs of yarn and rolled into a pile of pillows with a soft thud. Quickly followed by the bemused cackling of an also unraveling Dindet, as she too tumbled headlong into the stack of pillows.

Her head popped out of the mess and she waited while Oliver dug through himself, coming out with a gasp and wave of tasteful delight.

"Wh..what is this place?" He asked through a laugh, picking up one of the pillows to chunk at the clown in meager revenge for her little trick.

Dindet giggled upon impact and responded in kind.

"I don't know, I call it The Nursery though." She glanced from left to right with a sheepish grin and crawled over the pillows to whisper, "Do you wanna see why?"

"Sure, why not?" Oliver lightly smacked her in the face with another pillow and hoisted himself out of the pile to follow.

Dindet clasped his hand in hers and led him toward a large felt hill that dipped down into a small valley, hidden by more yarn bushes. And promptly shoved him into one of them, jumping in after.

"You gotta be real quiet, and real slow– otherwise they get scared." she whispered softly, reaching past him to push aside bundles of knots to reveal what dwelled at the base of the valley.

Oliver leaned forward to get a better look, and much to his delight, a herd of baby animals congregated around each other donning absurd pastel patterns like infantile toys.

"Oh. My. God." *Precious. All of them.* Immediately the urge to pet and hold and cuddle every single little animal crashed into the kid with the speed of a steam engine and he quickly scrambled out of the bush to try and win one over.

From afar, they looked like regular-sized baby animals, but as he approached he realized that these little pets were almost as big as cars and that really only made it harder not to dive headfirst into their soft fur.

Dindet followed more cautiously from behind, glancing around the valley to make sure nothing bad was lurking anywhere.

Oliver, on the other hand, had successfully rounded up a large duckling and harlequin rabbit and promptly shoved the entire front half of his body into their downy fur, content to simply let the large-small animals sit on him if it meant he could just be there for a while.

It was the best he felt in months, everything about this place– this dimension was so comforting. Like falling asleep on a cotton candy cloud except it was real and he was actually here.

He dropped down on the ground, relishing in the Minky fleece grass and letting all sorts of chicks, and kittens and bunnies and ducklings and puppies crawl over him as if he were just an unwitting carpet. This whole place was just so...warm.

"I do really like this place." Oliver mused from the ground, not even opening his eyes to look up at the sky despite the pink alligators flying above him like buzzing dragonflies. "How did you find it?"

Briefly, he opened an eye to look at the clown resting on the back of the black and white rabbit he had found earlier.

"I found it on my way of finding you...I think?" She answered, not really looking back at him, but instead at a small lake ahead of her that shimmered like an oil slick.

Oliver let out a content sigh, deciding it better not to ask why she wanted to find him- for all he cared, he could lie down and sleep here forever.

"Can you tell me how time travel works?" He asked instead, though it was for a slightly different reason this time. He hoped, maybe if she rambled long enough, he would fall asleep. He could always ask again later.

Dindet lackadaisically rolled over and off the rabbit, grabbing a thread of yarn from a bush and tugging it along with her.

"Okay," She said, taking the string and tying it loosely around one of his fingers. "Time is like this uh, yarn. It starts somewhere. Like your mini arm-arm."

"Finger?"

She pulled on the string, just enough to lift his hand a little and catch his attention. Oliver sat up and glanced down at the yarn and gave her an incredulous smile.

"You're not gonna wrap me up again are you?"

She shook her head, "Not unless you want me to?"

She continued, replicating the yarn to match all ten of his fingers, tying each one and spreading them out like a fan.

"What are you doing?" Oliver held his hands still, watching as the yarn she had tied continued to grow longer.

"I'm showing you how time works. See?" Dindet gestured at the threads, "all of them are different times and they all move at different speeds, but they always, only ever go forward."

He nodded slightly, taking another second to inspect the pieces of yarn. Each one started at different times from when she tied them, but the rate at which they grew varied greatly from one another. Which only meant one thing.

"So it's impossible to go backwards.."

"It's not impossible." She retorted, "it's just a really bad idea."

The clown fabricated a small pair of scissors and snipped one of the threads, causing the entire thing to unravel and fall off his thumb. She then took the thread and tied it into a ring.

"If you go back in the same timeline, it stops time from growing and makes a paradox- cause you did something that can't be undone. It's forced to start over." She handed the loop of yarn to Oliver and picked up another two pieces of thread.

"So, you have to go to a place where time moves different, sometimes it moves slower or faster than where your from, but it always moves forward." Dindet set down the thread and began untying them from his fingers, balling them up and throwing them over her shoulder with a soft smile. "If you go back in the same timeline, you have to keep going back over and over."

"It's better to move sideways in time instead of backwards. That's what I do."

The cheer in her voice didn't make his heart not drop at the notion. *It was a stupid idea anyway.*

"I didn't realize it was so strict," He replied quietly, keeping his eyes downward at his twiddling thumbs.

His sorrow crept in the air like a fog and Dindet quickly attempted to save face, tapping his shoulder and pointing at the small lake she was looking at earlier.

"Hey, you wanna fly?" She offered, garnering a confused look from him until he followed her finger to the lake which on occasion, spewed large bubbles that caught stray roaring dandelions in the air.

"Sure, that sounds nice." Oliver pulled himself to his feet and meandered toward the lake with the clown at his side, not really regaining any of the warmth he'd lost on the previous topic.

He never should have asked about it, really. There wasn't any point to try and go back, he just sounded like his dad and it was a stupid, hopeless task. Deep down he knew that, and he was sure Dindet did too.

"Actually...can we just go home?" He asked, slowing to a halt a few feet behind her.

Dindet turned and offered a gentle smile, trying very hard not to eat his sorrow and show him just how hollow he felt.

"Yeah, if you want to?" She popped to his side and obliged the request, waiting for him to look up to see that they were back in his room now, though the sun had set a while ago.

"My dad probably needs your help with his machine right now."

"...right."

The clown lingered for a moment in front of him, looking torn over whether or not she should actually leave. He didn't care though, other terribly dark things occupied his mind so much that he didn't even notice her leave.

It's been long enough so why does it still feel so empty? I should be used to it by now.

He didn't know, he didn't really want to. He stood alone in his room for a moment, feeling like his head was going to pop off his shoulders and float into the sky like a balloon, so he took a step forward. And another. And then a couple more. And when he looked up he was in a place that for a really long time, he didn't go.

His parents' room.

Not even his dad would go inside anymore, he slept on the couch or on the spare bed in the attic, and everything in there was the same as that day like it was a picture someone took.

They were going to go out for dinner to celebrate his 'birthday' as mom had said. She laid out a pretty dress, one he always thought made her look prettier than anyone else in the world. Better than her wedding dress even.

It was covered in dust.

Everything was. It even caught the light in the six-month-old glass of water on the nightstand on her side of the bed. The light had gone out in the sky, and the moon left a ghostly blue hue that made the dust in the air shimmer. *She was supposed to be here.*

She was supposed to come back. She was supposed to fix things.

Oliver stood at the side of the bed, staring blindly at it and feeling the hollowness he felt every time her name- anything about her was mentioned.

Deftly, he sifted through his pockets, in search of that awful little folded-up letter that had come in the mail weeks ago. What did it say...

'Dr. Jariwala, you've been summoned to appear in court to discuss the custody arrangements proposed by Mr. Matthew Tarsul. Federal law dictates that sole custody of the child is returned to the closest living relative after the prior custodial guardian has been declared deceased.

Lack of response will evolve into a civil dispute in court and the child, one Olivia Annere Tarsul will be removed and placed in the care of her current legal guardian until the dispute is resolved.'

He could cry, maybe, but at the same time he was still lost in a kind of whirling nightmare that ripped all semblance of tears away from him. It was just this nothingness that draped over him like a cold, dark, shadow, seeping into his lungs and keeping him from breathing. It was far worse than anything he could ever articulate.

Numbly, he reached forward, daring to disturb this self-made tomb, and stole the dress, sending little puffs of dust swirling in the air as he crawled onto the bed and clutched the forgotten garment close, digging his fingers into his skin in weak effort to not hurt in the same way all the time.

She was..she was supposed to be here...

None of this would happen if she were just..here.

Little Mouse

Dindet stood there in front of the boy for a moment, hoping that maybe he would somehow stop spiraling into the cold dark abyss that seemed to open up from underneath him. It tasted so familiar to her that she dare not take a bite or she would be entirely consumed herself.

This was so much harder than she could ever have imagined, not eating but getting just a little taste of all of it. It was like colors that flashed around her in a strobe that made holding herself together so much harder than it was supposed to be.

She could sate herself with other things on occasion, but the desire to devour every little thought he had was close to all-encompassing. Emotion radiated off of Oliver like a kaleidoscope of colors, constantly changing and always so terribly enticing.

"..Right.." She answered softly, respecting the hole that had begun devouring him and only hoping that it would lessen in size. He didn't look at her when she answered, and instead looked at the nothingness around her, wobbling on his feet in an unconscious fervor of quiet suffering.

It was very real, almost tangible to the clown, and she thought if he could see how dark inside he was, that maybe he would actually let her help like she was trying to. *It's all she came here to do, right?*

All she really wanted to do.

Of course, she didn't know or understand why that was, or why upon existence she felt such a fire inside to seek out someone she had never met before. It felt like something she would start the world over for.

It was the only thing that seemed to stave off starvation- no matter how hungry she became.

Dindet quietly turned away from him, doing as he suggested and making a small effort to help his father with the project he needed her for.

When she peeked through the slit in the door, she caught a glimpse of the machine, thinking it some kind of rudimentary attempt at mimicking her ability to vibrate her molecular structure.

Clearly it wasn't complete, otherwise the mushy remains of deconstructed mice wouldn't have been rotting in a trash can with their still alive brethren shrieking nearby.

There was a piece of her floating in a small jar, undulating in effort to return to its host and Jon stood hunched over a large blueprint, trying to decipher notes written by his wife.

"Hello?" She asked quietly, more hesitant than anything to call his attention, she didn't so easily forget the man's vengeful thoughts- even if they were never to be acted on.

The scientist bobbed his head up and down before turning to see who stood behind him.

"Dindet! Fantastic! Come here, I need your help deciphering these notes real quick." The man pressed a hand against her back and pushed the clown forward to look at a large piece of paper with white lines and scribbles all over it. she recognized most of it as human words and a few that she recognized as very much so not.

In a quick instant, she phased backward through her guide in a startled shuffle and tasted the sharp bitter sting of fear on her tongue, quickly shoving it into some deep recess of her mind to maintain her little facade.

"You recognize it?" Jon turned heel, catching what little hue hadn't been reverted yet, and swiftly stepped toward her. "You- you need to tell me what this says, Marie- my wife..she knew your people. She worked with you, I need to know how to find her!"

His voice raised as his desperation did, and he nearly shook her in his grip, only adding to Dindet's confusion and fear.

His thoughts bombarded her like rocks, crashing in and crushing through the static wall she had put up to hide from them.

Too much. Everything was *everywhere, all at once* and so much harder than before and she could barely hold it together.

The sheer force of his desperation compounded with the hole underneath Oliver that grew so dark and black it felt like it wanted to swallow her up and she wanted to- needed to go away. For just a little while.

For a brief moment, not to harm him, but only to make him let go, Dindet tore down her wall and let out the heinous shriek of terror that she let build up for days. Loud and painful and shocking enough, that the scientist ripped his hands away and tumbled backward, stopping himself at the table and frantically attempting to catch the cages of mice he knocked down.

He lowered, slowly, into a crouch and shuddered to himself, suddenly realizing what fresh alien horror he was really dealing with.

This wasn't a game. This wasn't his son or even human, he should have known better than to relate something that seemed so deceptively innocent to being entirely harmless.

His eye caught a small mouse, squealing from underneath a wrench that had landed on its foot. It must have scurried away when he knocked the cages loose. Jon reached out and cupped the little white rodent in his hand, gingerly lifting the tool and inspecting its crushed and bloody hind leg.

"I- I'm sorry, I didn't mean to startle you." He hesitantly shot a glance toward the clown, who stood at the far end of the room, a deep purple hue that slowly returned to form as calm began to come back to her.

"I should've realized that you're here of your own accord..not for us." He continued, standing up with the suffering animal in his palm.

Jon stepped around his table and made his way to his machine, setting the little mouse down on the wide platform and gesturing in hopes that Dindet would come closer.

He moved to the right of the machine, and pulled a lever, causing the contraption to whir to life and the electricity in the house to flicker in effort to conserve the power needed to run everything at once.

Sparks flew from two prongs on each side of the platform, arcing and connecting with a jolt of almost plasma as it attempted to tear a hole in space.

Dindet stood mortified by the thing, instantly realizing the capability of the machine. It was an abomination, a world-ending nightmare. *And clowns helped create it?!*

The little mouse squealed in terror at the dancing lights above it, meekly reaching out to try and escape until its little heart accepted the inevitability and the thing stilled itself. Breathing furiously and heavily as strikes of small lightning caged it in a glowing, burning, and what Dindet knew would be a terribly painful death.

With a zap and a flash and a little unintentional fire, what was meant to be a portal appeared, disappeared and the little mouse was nothing but a pile of congealed goo.

A low buzz and ticking noise sounded and the lights that had gone out began to regain their glow. Jon looked back at the clown who wore her horror plainly on her face.

In an instant, she popped to the edge of the hot plate of death and scooped the mushy little thing into her hands, trying desperately to parse out what all it was made of.

"It's no use. I've tried everything but I can't get it to work." Jon muttered solemnly, "They all turn out like that."

Dindet ignored him, cupping the what-once-was-a mouse in her hands and dissolving it further until she was sure she could manage it. She pressed her palms together until she felt a heartbeat, lungs, kidneys, intestines, soon the thing was like an infant in a womb, and then finally, she opened up her hands to reveal a very small, and very new baby mouse.

Jon's eyes widened at the miracle and he knelt down, ignoring how the clown flinched away slightly. He peered at the entirely new and yet resurrected organic lifeform she had created.

He was speechless, more than so, he almost couldn't understand what exactly allowed her to perform an almost godlike act.

"You don't have the properties to rebuild them." She said finally, taking the little mouse and setting it inside a new cage. "You need a piece of them to be able to find them, and you need enough of them to remake them."

Dindet phased past him and pointed at the open circuit board that had caught fire earlier.

"It's getting too hot too, you need something to keep it cool or you'll boil anything that you get to come through." She then gestured at the blueprints. "The notes say that it's not supposed to open a hole, it's supposed to just move matter- you built it all wrong, that's why it kills everything."

Jon nodded in somber confirmation, suddenly feeling far more guilt than before over the rodents he sent to their deaths in a machine that was built completely incorrectly.

"How do I build it correctly? Do you know?" A genuine question he never thought he would truly find the answer to, until now.

"You shouldn't build it at all..." it may have been calm, but the gravity of her voice made the man hesitant to argue.

"Please..." Jon knelt to Dindet's level and hesitantly, gently, placed a hand on her shoulder, only lifting it slightly when she flinched and turned a deep blue and starry black tears formed under her eyes. "I only need to use it once. Then I'll destroy it. I promise."

Dindet's eyes flickered from the machine back to the man as she desperately tried to eat as little as possible from him.

She let out a soft, reluctant sigh and closed her eyes in submission.

"I can...build it for you."

***

Majority of the night was spent disassembling Jon's death machine, though sleeplessness never really affected the clown.

To the scientist she was like a machine, never needing to stop and rest or to worry about forgetting to eat.

He was never more wrong, but Dindet preferred to keep her unorthodox way of refueling a secret. Perhaps because she was sated by something else. Definitely a little because she knew it would probably scare the two of them. Especially if they found out how terribly hungry she could get.

In the night, time in this dimension seemed to slow for a bit, even though it didn't really, she noticed that almost everything, even the sleepless scientist would slow to a crawl and eventually stop entirely, finding a comfortable place to lay his head on stacks of newly drawn blueprints and falling asleep.

When everything was still and quiet, she decided that now would be a good time to check on the hole underneath Oliver.

He had moved from his room when she popped in to look, but a little sniff was all that was needed to find out exactly where he went.

Hesitantly, she gripped the frame of a door that she hadn't explored yet, and peeked through. He was curled up in a small little ball of a boy on a bed that was twice his size, wrapped up in some dark fabric that smeared particles of dust on the clothes he didn't change out of.

The hole wasn't gone, but it was smaller. Dindet couldn't exactly figure why, but she also didn't want to because, on some level, she knew that it was a very painful thing to have inside you at all.

In his sleep, the boy rolled and stretched, murmuring to himself something inaudible that she was sure wasn't an actual word. She didn't want to disturb this rhythm that seemed to be required of the creatures here, so she quietly departed, making the decision instead to sit outside on the porch where the fuzzy, food-named cats liked to tress about in the dark.

She liked them, and they seemed to like her, as every time she came nearby they would crawl up from various hiding spots to mewl and press their faces into her body in effort to garner attention.

It was cold here, and she wasn't sure why they found comfort in her because she knew that staying outside would mean she would reach a freezing point and be more of a rock than a pet provider. Maybe they simply liked to sit in her lap and around her because on some level she resembled a human being.

She wasn't afraid of freezing or being alone in the dark. Mostly, she was comfortable with the silence, and she greatly enjoyed the stars in the sky. Though she knew that was just her.

Really, she only came outside to keep an eye on the lines of tall trees just past the backyard. They would come for her. She didn't know when, or how, what would happen when they got here, but they would come and she needed to be prepared.

"What are you doing?" Oliver's groggy voice floated out over the still and frosty air.

Did the sky circle rise already?

Dindet cracked and shuddered off the thin layer of ice that

molded around her throughout the night in order to turn and look at him.

He was already in new clothes and far less empty looking now. The hole wasn't gone though. It seemed ever so slightly bigger, actually.

"Did you sit out here all night?" He yawned, waving for her to come back inside for breakfast.

Dindet glanced around, noticing that the cats were all swarming their food bowls now, which meant they would leave soon.

Quietly, she stood up, shaking off the last of the ice before following Oliver back into the house.

"Do you want any cereal?" He offered as he pulled down a bowl and a box of small sparkly square-shaped chips of homogenized wheat and cinnamon.

"I don't have a stomach," Dindet answered rather blandly, watching him pour an extra bowl and shove it toward her anyways.

"So? People are going to think something is wrong with you if you don't eat like a person." He hoisted himself onto a stool and began crunching down on his own bowl, staring off at the living area in silence.

Something about him wasn't right at all.

Not in the sense that Dindet recognized at least. On occasion, she got a whiff of the empty, and when she peered over at him it looked like he was trying very hard not to cry. Then, he would blink a few times and sit more upright, sucking in a breath through his nose before taking another silent bite from his spoon.

It was disconcerting if she knew what that word meant. Of course, she was far too hesitant to mention it due to the little pattern she had discovered in his kaleidoscope of colors. So instead, she got up on a stool as well and began shoving large spoonfuls into the hole in her face in effort to mimic him.

She would decide what to do with the material later.

Some Things Take More Time

"So, as you can see, based on these studies, elemental particles, like these electrons, only follow the laws of physics when observed, and while we haven't quite figured out why, it's quite an interesting notion considering the vastness of the universe and everything we can't really see in it!" Mr. Chavez rambled on, pausing the video he'd set up for the class to watch for the past thirty minutes. However, Oliver was far more preoccupied with doodling in his sketchbook than learning about electrons.

At least, until the principal quietly stepped into the classroom and pulled all the students' attention away from the screen.

He whispered something to the teacher and gestured vaguely toward the class with a nod.

"Mr. Tarsul, you're requested in the office? Someone is on the phone for you." Mr. Chavez drew the kid's attention away from his half-finished drawing and Oliver made a face, something between confusion and annoyance.

It doesn't make sense for anyone to call the school just for me.

Dad usually just called the phone or sent a text. The only time-

The only time anyone ever called the school for me was when the accident happened.

Dindet's attention twisted away from her attempt at writing notes, and her head shot up at the horrid flavor of anxiety that seemed to suddenly jut out of Oliver like a thousand little spikes. He didn't say anything though, and moved like nothing was wrong at all.

Though every other student's eyes clashed up against him, almost expecting it to be something bad.

"What do you bet it's AKAN telling him he's officially an orphan?" Theo snidely remarked, making sure to keep her voice too quiet for the teacher to overhear.

"That's really not funny," Cassidy chided, though even she swirled up with a ripple of colors at the devastating idea.

Dindet leaned over toward Douglass in meager effort to get his attention, "What does she-"

"Mr. Chavez, can I use the restroom please?" The boy interrupted, abruptly standing up and barely even glancing back at the clown.

"Go grab the pass." The teacher waved him off, but before Douglass made his move to leave, he felt the smallest of tugs on his shirt, abetting him to hesitate.

Dindet stared at him, and for a second her eyes flickered toward the door as if she knew he wasn't actually going to the restroom.

"It's nothing, I just wanna check in on him is all," Douglass offered a smile, the kind that made you look more sad than happy. It complemented the torrent of worry that seemed to swell inside him and paint the room yellow, in the few short moments that Oliver had been away.

***

Oliver meandered down the hall, stopping every couple of feet to contemplate turning around, while still managing to reassure himself that it wasn't bad. *Dad was home, it's probably Chris from the lab checking to ask when he'd come back to work.*

But that doesn't really make sense, he could just text him, right? Maybe it is Dad? Calling to say he finished his project? No, they just started rebuilding the whole thing. It was nothing, probably, at most, it might be aunt Manpreet or Baba on a collect call from India? It had been a while since they checked in, and they tend to call the school instead of my cell phone anyways.

"Hey, uh, someone said there's a call for me?" Oliver opened the office door mid-sentence, pulling Mrs. Deauxtree's attention away from her computer for the moment. The woman looked him up and down, slowly coming to the realization that the kid was, in fact, there for something.

"Oh, yeah, it's your father, he just wanted to check in on you? I've had him on hold." That was more than a relief to hear.

The lady practically bounced in her chair over toward the phone, picking the whole thing up and setting it on the counter so he could reach it easier. Oliver picked up the phone and held it up to his ear, praying that it had something to do with the project, a breakthrough, something good.

"Yeah, Dad?" He answered, waiting for the reply through the muffled static of the other line.

"Olivia."

Oliver drew in a staggered breath and his stomach immediately twisted up in knots. His fingers clenched tightly around the phone until he could feel his pulse against the plastic.

"Wh-what do you want?" He attempted to steel himself in his words as if the mere sound of his biological father's voice didn't make every part of him want to hide.

"You changed your cell number, I've been trying to get a hold of you."

"We have a restraining order against you." He answered,

gritting his teeth in effort to keep them from chattering. "What is this? Your one free call from prison?"

"I'm not in prison, never was. And the restraining order was for your mother, not you. Why are you being so rude to me, Olivia?" The voice on the other end condescended, "I just wanted to talk to my pretty little girl, see how she was doing. Make sure that everything is okay. Since I didn't get to see her at the funeral. Or any other visitation for that matter."

"I don't want to talk to you," Oliver answered, readying himself to hang up the call.

"Wait-"

He stopped and hesitantly put the phone back to his ear.

"Don't you hang up on me young lady, I know you know why I called. And don't think for a second I won't come find you. I know where you're staying, I know where you go to school. You are my daughter. And you-"

Oliver slammed the phone down on the hook, harder than he actually intended, but enough to draw Mrs. Deauxtree's attention back to him and his far too erratic breathing.

"S-sorry, my hand slipped," He muttered, spinning on his heel to leave as quickly as possible.

"Is everything okay-"

"Yeah! Yeah- I'm, everything is fine." He cut in, already closing the glass door behind him.

He needed somewhere, a place to be, to hide. To get rid of all the terrible pent-up anxiety and fear that practically turned him into lead upon ending that awful phone call.

It's falling apart. Everything was falling apart, and if he wasn't careful, he would too. So he needed a place to be. Right now.

Oliver slid behind the door to the restroom and quickly moved to the biggest stall. The second he managed to fumble the door locked, it felt like every single pound of his stress and worry landed right on top of him, and he fell back against the wall, slowly sliding down to the floor in a terrible shaking mess.

This is bad, this is really bad.

***

Douglass rounded the corner, headed straight toward the main office, hoping to see the person he was looking for. He wasn't there though and probably was already on his way back to class. It was only a hunch, obviously.

But he knew that the last time Oliver had a phone call waiting for him, he got really bad news. And Douglass knew for a fact that was all the boy was probably thinking about.

As much as he usually tried to ignore it, Douglass had a particular soft spot for him. Despite Oliver being more than a little standoffish about it.

He could be mean, and inconsiderate. A lot of the time he was.

However, there was a gentle little memory burned into Douglass's head.

About a year or so ago, when he turned thirteen, he invited the kid to his Bar Mitzvah. And he only did it cause his dad suggested it, Oliver had only recently moved in with Jon at the time, and he went by Olivia.

Douglass could practically smell the flowery perfume he used to wear on a daily basis as if it somehow masked the way the kid looked so hollow. And afraid.

Even the bright red saree he wore, that horribly clashed with the other formal attire at the party, didn't cover up the way the kid twitched and jumped and hid away in the corners of the room, essentially walling himself off from anyone around.

Douglass casually pushed the bathroom door open, finally deciding to actually utilize the coveted bathroom pass he managed to get. Though, his reminiscing came to an abrupt halt the second he heard a semi-startled scrambling from one of the stalls.

"S-sorry!" He sputtered, already turning heel and hoping it wasn't two of the older kids doing something they really shouldn't.

"What do you want, Douglass?" Oliver's voice croaked through the large stall. His tone indicated some sort of disdain, though it was almost immediately betrayed by the exasperated quivering of his voice.

He stopped and glanced along the bottom gap between the floor and the stall doors. In the very last one, he could see the kid's legs, sprawled out on the floor like he had been sitting there for a while. Until they pulled back from his line of sight.

"I just came to..." he contemplated lying, "I wanted to see if you were okay."

"I don't want your pity."

Douglass rolled his eyes and dropped down on his hands and knees, crawling past the stalls until he peeked through the big one where Oliver was.

He was curled up in the corner, resting his head against the cold plastic wall and staring at the little dents other students had made with pens. His hands wrapped so tightly around his arms that Douglass could see the whites of his knuckles. The thing that made him move though, was how red and blotchy Oliver's face was. Like all he'd done for the past few minutes was cry.

Douglass let out a tiny little huff and promptly shoved himself halfway under the locked stall, pulling Oliver's attention away from the wall as he grunted and groaned his way into the tiny little room.

"Haven't you ever heard of privacy?!" Oliver spat, though he still adjusted himself to give the kid enough room to join him. "What is wrong with you?!"

"What's wrong with you?" Douglass repeated the question back, though the nature of it made the boy clamp his mouth shut and quickly turn away from him.

"None of your business."

Douglass nodded, he already knew that. And knew that if Oliver was going to say anything, it probably wasn't going to be for a while. Still though.

"You don't have to tell me if you don't want to." He said, leaning up against the wall next to him. "I don't mind just sitting here until you're ready to come back to class."

He didn't. And he didn't mind skipping class altogether if it meant that his friend wouldn't be okay.

"I don't need you to be there for me," Oliver muttered, refusing to look at him. He probably thought he was nosy, a pain. Some perpetual mistake that took more than enough pity on him. *Or maybe I just want to, have you ever thought of that?*

"I know you don't," Douglass remarked as if it didn't even phase him. "I just wanna be here. Bathrooms are infinitely more cool than AP physics."

Oliver didn't answer, and only really closed further in on himself. It reminded him of that day, and all he could really think about was the way he looked at his Bar Mitzvah.

There was always something so soft and fragile, hidden deep underneath all the armor that kid wore. Douglass almost admired him for it. No, he did admire him for it.

Oliver walked around with nasty, awful rumors floating around him, almost everywhere he went, and it made him cold and calloused, angry and mean. He walked around, looking like someone you didn't want to mess with, and that's the way he made himself look.

But behind that, there was always this scared little kid in a bright red saree, covered in fruit punch. Crying and shaking underneath the synagogue stairs.

And Douglass was pretty sure he was the only one who saw that. He was pretty sure even Oliver was blind to it or at least didn't see himself the way he should.

Oliver's eyes flickered back toward the kid. "Why do you do stuff like this? Act all nice to me when you know I'm not nice back?" He questioned, not even remotely contemplating the way the words could have landed on his ears.

"Cause I don't care," Douglass answered. Oliver blinked, and a frown split his face for a second or two as he registered what that meant.

"But I don't want you here."

"Then I'll go." Douglass smiled and got to his feet, but not much further the second the other boy's hand caught his shirt, beckoning him back.

"Wait- don't," Oliver quickly let go, and dropped his gaze to the floor. "I'm not...ready yet."

"To go back?"

He nodded, still staring at the ground as his friend dropped down next to him once more.

"I had.." Oliver paused, still not entirely sure why he wanted to tell Douglass so badly about what happened. "I had bad pictures in my- in my head."

"Yeah?" Douglass drew in a soft breath, his mind returning to the terrible sight his friend was in that red saree. Shaking, crying, and heaving empty breaths as if they were the last he would ever take. But it was nothing compared to the calmness that followed afterward.

Like nothing had happened at all like all those awful pictures didn't mean anything.

Douglass's thoughts ceased as a gentle pressure landed against his shoulder and he glanced down. Oliver's eyes were closed and he had rested up against him in their quiet.

"It's alright," Douglass murmured, resting his head against the wall, "it's over now."

"....yeah..."

On the Fritz

One of the first things Dindet noticed about this world—aside from how strange it was, was the level of routine that existed here.

It was almost the same thing as the day prior, but only a couple things had changed.

For instance, the Douglass boy tasted like cherries and would turn almost as red as one when she caught his eye. He seemed to make a point to avoid her entirely and he and Oliver walked at a much faster pace, despite Oliver making a concerted effort to be further away from him.

He also decided to sit next to him on the big rectangular box with wheels as opposed to the warm friendliness he had shown her yesterday as well.

Oliver on the other hand was having next to none of it. He didn't know why Douglass was hanging around him like an eager toddler and honestly didn't want to. It was weird, he was being weird.

He was constantly opening and closing his mouth like he wanted to say something, but not actually spitting it out. Or looking over his shoulder at the clown and making really dumb faces at Oliver, like he could somehow telepathically understand what was going on in his head.

It wasn't until the bus pulled into the schoolyard and the three of them got off that Douglass not very discreetly pulled him away from Dindet's immediate sight to actually make sense of his annoyingly odd behavior.

"Hey, I brought something to school today," Douglass whispered, glancing nervously around to make sure the new girl wouldn't see them.

Oliver raised an eyebrow. *Why does this matter?*

"Okay?"

Douglass squirmed under his gaze before reaching into his backpack to pull out the machine his dad let him borrow.

"Well, since she was so good at sciency stuff I figured I'd show her something cool my dad made— I figured you would think it was cool.." Douglass pulled Oliver toward the lockers, shielding his little contraption from the clown who was now conversing rather distractedly with Cassidy.

"Why is this important?" Oliver rolled his eyes at the boy's superfluous effort to hide something that really only made the two of them more suspicious.

Douglass looked just about like he was going to implode at the question.

"Well, I mean...I don't know what most girls like and you used to be one, so I figured if you thought it was cool then maybe Dindet would, and I could show her but also I didn't know if maybe you liked her too and I didn't want to—"

"I'm sorry *what?*" Oliver cut in with more than a little bit of anxious laughter.

Did he seriously just say what he said? Out loud?

Douglass folded in on himself like he wanted to look smaller than he was.

"Well, I mean...I figured I'd ask just in case."

Okay, okay, but what on God's green earth gave him the idea that he would— of course.

Oliver glanced back at the clown as he began to develop a little bit of an idea. He smacked Douglass's back lightly with a knowing smile.

"Douglass, I gotta say, I'm proud of you. Going out of your way to try and impress someone you don't even know." *And maybe get her off my back.* "It's very, uh, chivalrous. I think...I think you should wait for the perfect moment to strike."

He spun the unknowing pawn around in order to push him toward the classroom and let go with a false confidence-inducing finger gun.

"Maybe lunchtime?"

Oliver waited for some small confirmation that showed how Douglass fell into his little ploy and once it came, retreated toward the classroom, just as Cassidy and Dindet entered and the final bell trilled.

Most of class was boring, on occasion, Dindet would prod him with a finger to ask a stupid question, and in between class switches, Douglass would make winks and gestures that under normal circumstances would probably be cause for concern. It kind of looked like he was having a seizure.

Of course, Oliver played into his excitement and returned the overtly obvious winks with only the intention of gathering up this poor kid's feelings and bestowing them on one of the most annoying and aggravating things known to man.

To him, they were meant for each other.

Finally, as if descended from heaven itself, the moment came and the lunch bell rang, finally allowing all of them to depart to the cafeteria and for Oliver to witness what he was sure to be a spectacular end to his troubles.

If the two of them hit it off, they would- with maybe some

help, become entirely engrossed with each other and the only time he would ever have to be even remotely around Dindet would be when she was up in the attic fixing his dad's machine.

Dindet copied Oliver as he filed through the line, grabbing all the things he did and setting them all in the same places, and eventually following him to one of the hexagonal tables that littered the otherwise large room full of human children.

Last time, no one aside from the two of them sat at the table. However, this time around, both Douglass and the girl she'd spoken to earlier today slid into seats next to them, almost filling out the table's six sides.

She still hadn't decided what to do with the cinnamon toasts she haphazardly shoved inside her a day ago, and now she was faced with an audience- all of which ate like Oliver.

"So Oliver, Dindet said you helped her with reading last night?" Cassidy began, taking a quaint bite out of a plastic cup of mashed potatoes. "I wish you told me English wasn't her first language, cause I would have been happy to help."

She lowered her voice slightly, almost to the point it was under her breath, "But you didn't answer my texts, so I had to ask her this morning how your parts of the project were going."

Cassidy was like a mom, but not in the kind of way that made you enjoy her. She almost always had something to say. She was smart and pretty and a lot of the boys at school liked her because she had an accent, pretty hair, and her dark skin was paramount to flawless.

Course, no one actually tried to date her because her moms looked like they would burn anyone who attempted alive. And, also because she made everyone around her look really stupid in comparison.

She was nice though, and one of the only people who actually cared about him after the accident, even if he didn't want her to.

Oliver shrugged in ambivalence and pulled out his phone to

check for any texts. Yep, six texts from Cassidy's number, and one or two from an unknown.

He opened the two from the unknown number and promptly deleted them, not even taking the moment needed to see who they were from. He already knew.

"You're gonna eat right?" she asked a little louder, pointing an accusatory fork toward Dindet, who was focused on the amalgamation of tastes only she could sense, not the food that sat untouched on the tray in front of her.

"Oh, right," the clown answered distractedly and grabbed the slice of pizza on her tray, and stuffed it in her mouth, swallowing with one gulp. She glanced at Oliver, who pressed his palm to his forehead in embarrassment.

"Hey, Douglass, why don't you show Dindet that cool thing you showed me?" He changed the subject, prompting the boy to practically jump out of his seat in anticipation.

"It's really cool, Dindet, my dad made it– he's a scientist at the lab like Oliver's." Douglass reached into his backpack and whipped out a remote-looking contraption, pridefully holding it toward the clown to see.

Dindet cocked her head, her eyes flickering back to Oliver in silent confusion.

"It's an electromagnetic frequency thingy. I don't remember exactly what it does but my dad made this small one as a prototype for a new reusable energy source." Douglass explained, wagging it in front of her before pulling it back to mess with it.

"Don't you think it's a bad idea to bring your dad's work stuff to school?" Cassidy intruded fervently, though Douglass flagrantly ignored her, instead trying to figure out how to turn the thing on.

"It's not dangerous, he said it doesn't get enough energy to store or to power stuff, it's not like a taser or anything," he argued, pressing a button and causing the little toy to beep and blink as a little spark zapped inside a glass tube.

To demonstrate even further how harmless it was, Douglass pressed his finger into one of the antennae of the device.

"See? Doesn't hurt, now you try." He offered it to Cassidy and the girl shrank away with a look of mild disgust before intrigue took over. She hesitated, before closing her eyes and gently touching the antennae with the tip of her finger.

"Oh! Okay! It's like a little tingly sensation," she remarked, "Oliver, you try it."

Douglass offered the contraption to him, and he reluctantly obliged. It didn't really feel like anything except maybe like if you put your tongue to a battery but instead that happened on your finger.

"It's alright." He shrugged, looking at Dindet to see if she might try it too.

"You wanna?" Douglass smiled at the clown, who looked more than intrigued by the contraption. Hesitantly, Dindet poked the tip of the antennae and if Oliver didn't know better, most would have thought she simply shuddered.

A ripple ran up the tip of her finger and disrupted her entire facade like one of those turnstile billboards, but only for a barely noticeable split second until she froze entirely.

Oliver quickly and discreetly reached for her hand under the table to see if she was thinking something because she looked like she had become a stone-cold statue sitting in the chair. *Nothing.*

Oh no. Nothing is bad.

It wasn't even static, just nothing, and it wasn't like he knew exactly what just happened. He just knew it wasn't good.

"Dindet?" Douglass lowered the remote, his heart suddenly dropping to his feet.

"Is she okay?" Cassidy leaned in closer, inspecting the girl to try and figure out what just happened. "I– I don't think she's breathing, we need to call the—"

"No! No, she does this sometimes!" Oliver stammered,

jumping out of his chair to try and scoot the frozen alien away from the table. *Geeze, how is she so heavy?*

"Are you su—"

"Yeah! No, I mean– she has a condition, I just gotta call my dad. It's nothing to worry about, I swear!" Oliver dragged the chair and the clown along with it as best he could away from the table, stopping every couple of steps to breathe. "I'll take her...heh, to the nurse, don't worry about it."

"Maybe we should help?" Douglass weakly offered.

"No! I've got this!" Oliver retorted, finally getting the clown outside of the cafeteria so he could figure out what the heck was going on.

He crouched down to get a better look at her. She was entirely catatonic, frozen stiff— no, solid?

Oliver nervously poked her, hoping that if he pressed hard enough he would pop the weird film bubble that hid all her star goop. Nothing but solid rock, it felt like he was just shoving his finger into a brick wall.

With increasing frantic, he whipped out his phone and dialed his dad, hoping that for the love of all that is holy, he was awake.

"Hrrrrrrmm" *Close enough.*

"Dad, I need you to come get us, the clown turned into a rock." He whispered harshly into the phone.

"Shheee...frrrh..innowhat?" There was a shuffle and a loud crash followed by screeching mice.

"She's not moving or doing anything, I— I don't know what to do, but she's really heavy and I can't move her alone, and I– I can't take her to the nurse!" His voice cracked with his increasing anxiety and he quickly spun around in a little circle to make sure no one was around.

"Hrrrralroght." It would be best to assume that was a yes.

Oliver hung up and glanced around once more, the bell would ring soon and he would need to find somewhere to shove this statue of an alien. *Where..where?*

His eye caught what he imagined to be a miracle, the janitorial closet that had a broken lock. It never closed all the way but no one except the seniors went inside to skip class and make out. It was perfect.

Only problem was that it was about twenty feet from where he stood and it would take a while and considerable strength to get rock freak from here to there.

Oliver sprinted to the closet and pulled it open. *No seniors, good.*

He then sprinted back and began the trek, hoping the lunchroom chatter was drowning out the high-pitched squeal of metal chair legs dragging along linoleum tiles.

The clown was extraordinarily heavy, it was almost like he was trying to pull a two hundred pound block, except it looked like a girl no bigger than an eighth-grader. It didn't help that her hand was outstretched in a way that if he accidentally lost his grip the whole thing might actually snap off and crumble.

More than halfway there.

Oliver caught a glimpse of one of the teachers milling the halls with her head thoroughly shoved in a cheezy romance novel and quickly stopped, tipping Dindet back on all legs and making up some dumb conversation.

"Yeah, that's the trophy case, tons of great achievements for Pineton Blizzards—" He watched intently as the teacher passed, waiting for her to turn down another hall toward the teachers' lounge before returning to his efforts.

Finally, with one last tug, he managed to thwart the odds and secure a hiding spot inside the closet. He grabbed a spare bucket and turned it over to use as a seat, resituating the clown so that he could watch her and peek through the crack in the door at the same time.

Way to ruin everything Dindet. Stupid clown. How was I

supposed to know that was gonna happen?

He glared at her dumb, confused face, letting out a little disgruntled huff at his perpetual suffering.

"You screwed up everything," He muttered, looking her up and down to see if anything changed. *Probably shouldn't have told Douglass to show her that thing.* "You're so stupid. You shouldn't have touched it."

Oliver pulled out his phone, nothing from his Dad. He peeked through the door, lunch wasn't over yet. *Stupid freaking alien should have known better, or this— whatever it is, wouldn't have happened.*

"You wouldn't have gotten hurt if you didn't mess with it. You don't even know what it does." He bit softly, bopping the clown on the head quite gently.

She didn't move or respond, and it made his nerves worse. She just sat there, staring at nothing, pointing at nothing, like she died and went into rigor mortis. *She wasn't dead though. She couldn't be. Could she?*

Oliver gasped unconsciously at the thought and reached out to touch her again. Just to try and maybe hear if she were thinking at all. *She would be okay. It would be fine. This was alright. I don't need to worry— it's not like I care at all.*

I don't care! I don't care about her at all- obviously. Why would I? She's been ruining my life, she took away mom. This was her fault. All of this..is- is supposed to be her fault.

Excuses Excuses

After an hour or two, Oliver heard his name called over the intercom, followed by Dindet's, and then his phone began buzzing violently.

"Dad?" He answered, hiding the stress in his voice.

"Where are you guys?"

"Janitor closet outside the cafeteria. She still hasn't changed." He answered quietly, peaking out of the crack in the door to see his father's dirty lab coat flash by. The door swung open and Jon stared down at him in tired confusion and worry.

"I don't– don't know what happened!" Oliver stammered as he got to his feet to help his dad hoist the frozen alien into the air to better carry her to the car.

"It's fine, son." Jon did a quick look around the hall, catching sight of a few cameras. "Remind me to hack the security system later."

His dad did more of the heavy lifting than Oliver, so the kid sprinted forward to put down the back seat in order to fit both the clown and the chair she was fused to inside.

Oliver got into the passenger seat and quietly waited for his father to adequately shove the alien into the back before he slammed the trunk shut and got into the driver's seat.

"How long has she been like this?" Jon asked as he set the car into drive and left the parking lot.

"I don't know? Since about noon?" Part of him wished he had kept a better track of time.

"Figured," Jon remarked, as he took a few turns down a back road that would get them home a little faster.

"You woke me up with the call and I noticed that this.." Jon pulled his sample jar out of his pocket and dropped it into Oliver's lap to look at. "Was like that."

The piece of the clown he had taken was a perfect cube, entirely solid, knocking around in the jar with loud little clinks.

"Figured whatever it was that happened, converted the matter into a complete solid."

Finally, they pulled up to the cabin, and Oliver jumped out to open the trunk while his dad made his way over to the porch to grab a spare dolly.

"If you get in on the other side and tip her over this way, I think I can catch her in this and it'll be a lot easier to lift her into the house." His father directed, situating the dolly just so that when Oliver climbed into the back seat in front of Dindet, he could easily tip her backward and she would land headfirst into the dolly, and hopefully not break on impact.

Once they successfully carted the alien inside, there wasn't much more to do aside from wait. She was ridiculously heavy, so Oliver just left her in the living room while he tried to figure out an excuse for Douglass and Cassidy. If they were keen to poke and prod, he needed something more than 'random freezing condition'

This is abysmal.

A couple more hours ticked by, all while Jon tried to figure out why whatever happened, happened, and Oliver glided between nigh engulfing rage and something he preferred not to state as genuine worry.

Because he didn't care. Obviously.

He paced from his room down toward the clown before stopping at the edge of the stairs and deciding that it wasn't meant to be important and backtracking toward the attic instead.

"Still nothing," Oliver muttered as he barged through the door to see his dad engrossed in some schematics of his machine.

"It's gonna be fine, Ols, you don't need to worry," he answered, not looking up from his work.

"I'm not." He grumbled quietly before turning to leave just as the doorbell rang.

Jon looked up and made quick eye contact with his son. *Not good.*

Oliver trampled back downstairs, frantically pausing for a moment while he searched for something to hide the clown with. *Sheets? A blanket? The couch quilt!*

He ripped the quilt off of the couch and draped it over the clown before answering the increasingly frequent ringing at the door.

"Yeah?" Oliver cracked the door open, coming face to chest with Mr. Furkin.

"Olivi— Oliver? Is your step-father home? I came to apologize about what happened. Douglass told me he accidentally zapped your friend and triggered a seizure?" The slightly distraught scientist pulled the door open further and pushed past Oliver into the house without so much as a 'thank you'. Instead, he searched the area in effort to find his colleague and perhaps Dindet.

Luckily, he didn't seem to be very observant of his surroundings and walked right past her as he went up the stairs to find Jon.

Oliver let out the breath he had been holding unconsciously and glanced back at the shrouded alien, noticing something uncomfortably peculiar.

The quilt was slowly turning black with an inky stain that

trailed and dripped onto the floor, like a puddle of molten jello.

He quickly pulled off the quilt, revealing a gruesome-looking melting black mold of the clown that lurched haphazardly like a quickly thawing ice sculpture, except as she melted little flecks of cinnamon toast cereal poked out from the tar-like goop, followed by an entirely undigested pizza slice and finally a rather disgusting leaking trail of milk.

"Gross." Oliver whinged, lifting his feet to try and avoid the goo as it began to spread. There was a lot more of it than he initially imagined, but it was mostly like a congealed jelly that sluggishly pooled around the chair, leaving behind just a little orange oval amidst the bits of milky pizza and cereal.

"Is she doing alright? I feel awful— I never should have let him take it..." Mr. Furkin's voice sounded from the upstairs hall as Oliver caught sight of movement from the doorway.

Do something! Now!

He ripped open the drawers and cabinets, pulling out a large gumbo pot and a ton of pans and bowls, and began scraping bits and pieces of the gel into the dishes. After lifting them as best he could onto the stove, he quickly scavenged some dish towels to soak up whatever was left just in case, and scrambled to take the quilt to the laundry room all before Mr. Furkin made it downstairs.

The scientist took a peek at the pot on the stove, making a rather disgusted look just as Oliver rounded the corner.

"What are ya cookin?" He asked with a gentle smile.

Lie. Find something to say.

"Oh, Dindet wasn't feeling so well, so I'm making a..." Oliver's eyes flickered back at the pot, as a cloud of smoke began floating up from it. "A— uh, traditional soup from her culture?"

Mr. Furkin stared at him for a moment, almost long enough to make the boy question if the lie worked.

"Sounds sweet of you." He shrugged his shoulders and put his hands in his pocket. "I was going to invite you guys to dinner as an apology but if she's still not feeling great we can reschedule."

"It– it's fine, really." Oliver offered a more than nervous smile as he slapped a lid on the smoking pot. "I'm sure once things cool down we can stop by."

The scientist nodded, lingering far longer than Oliver wanted him to, but it wasn't really like he had a choice in the matter.

"So..how have things been since.."

"It's alright!" Oliver put a little more weight on the lid of the pot as the pressure built up inside. "Things are going pretty great—awesome actually, Dad's working on a new project and it's really helping him out with everything."

Mr. Furkin nodded once again, offering a consoling smile.

"Yeah... speaking of which, I have some information for him I forgot to mention earlier."

Oh, thank god.

Mr. Furkin gave a small salute before heading back towards the attic and allowing Oliver to lift just a little bit of the pressure on the gas Dindet had converted to. The release caused the lid to nearly fly into the ceiling as the smoke swirled up and wafted into the air, hanging like a thick black fog in the kitchen.

***

Mr. Furkin made his way back up toward the attic, interrupting the work Jon was doing with a meek knock on the door frame.

"I meant to ask, how are things going?" He said gently as he stepped over various rolls of paper and tools scattered around the floor.

"What? Everything is fine Chris, why?" Jon didn't seem to hear him or understand. Chris glanced around the room, it was a horrible mess. It reeked of mouse feces and urine, blueprints and schematics littered just about every inch of the place and the only way to get to the guest bed was by serpentine path through stacks of cages, a half turned chalkboard, and a large metal machine that looked to be just in the beginnings of creation.

"You haven't been back to work in six months, I suddenly get an email from you about tracking radiation and hacking the lab? And this? With Olivia— Oliver, going through whatever is happening...and now you're taking care of another kid? It doesn't look good Jon." Chris solemnly gestured around the room. "*This* doesn't look good."

Jon shook his head and jerked up from his work, clamoring over heaps of trash to get to his chalkboard to maybe try and give some kind of explanation.

"I'm so close though, look, see?" He turned the board over showing calculations so horrible looking they resembled a child's handwriting. "I scavenged her blueprints, schematics, functions— everything and I– I can rebuild it. I can find her and bring her back."

There was a hope and desperation in his voice that wrenched Chris's heart as he tried to empathize with the man. He was just..so lost. He set a hand on Jon's shoulder with a heavy reluctant sigh.

"I'll do what I can to help."

Chris lowered his eyes as his colleague seemed to entirely ignore him. This place was such a mess, it was a miracle anything in here worked. It looked like he never left.

Chris's eye caught something sitting inconspicuously on the table, a small jar with a black gas inside that seemed to float from one side to the other.

"What's this?" he asked, picking up the jar to inspect the strange material further, it looked like nothing he had ever seen before. Or rather nothing he believed he'd seen.

"Just something I've been testing," Jon answered busily, not interested in that more than the equations the clown had created to explain the best way to build his way back to Marie.

Chris closely observed as the gas began to undulate in a perfect ring that continuously rippled outward.

"Did– did it just become a state of BEC?" Chris stared at the sample as it transformed slowly from one state of matter to the next until it finally settled on some odd floating jelly-like colloid. "Can I test this?"

"Sure, sure— lemme just..."Jon waved in dismissal of the request and turned to his machine, entirely occupied by reconnecting loose and misplaced wires.

Chris obliged and quietly set the small jar in his pocket, and sounded his departure before heading down the stairs, catching Oliver trying to shove something large and heavy into the pantry.

"Catch you later." He smiled, before finally leaving the house.

Oliver pressed himself against the pantry door as the creature inside pushed against it, beginning to seep through the cracks, only letting up once Mr. Furkin was well and gone.

The force from inside the pantry spewed out, thrusting the boy into the island as the door swung open and a gooey mock-up of Dindet quietly stepped out to do something that he was sure to regret as soon as he figured out what it was.

The semi corporeal creature sludged around the kitchen into the living room, slowly regaining some form of solidity as color and feature returned to it, and the much more familiar clown stood in front of the couch looking far more confused than ever.

"How long was I out?"

"You were— you were uncONCIOUS?!" Oliver seethed, digging his hands into his hair before he began to flail in a frustrated rampage around the room.

"Do you have ANY idea how hard it is to deal with you?!" He began, shooting glares back at her as he gestured at a slowly resolving puddle of goo on the floor, followed by the undigested food sitting in the chair.

"I'm sorry, I didn't mean to—"

"I don't CARE if you didn't *MEAN* to! I had to cover for you! I had to hide you and I had no idea what happened!" He cut her off, raising his voice until it nearly cracked as he yelled at her.

The clown turned a deep purple as she nervously backed away from him, trying to come up with an answer— a reason, maybe, to calm him down. But she couldn't find words at all, so instead, she lowered her eyes in guilt as he continued to chastise her.

"How can you just stand there looking stupid?! Do you have any idea how worried—"

Oliver cut himself off, realizing all too slowly how terrified she looked, how she shrank down in front of him.

"Just..be more careful." He quieted, dropping his aggressive posture and folding back in on himself in order to ease some of the tension. "I thought you might have gotten hurt...or something."

He hesitantly glanced back at the clown to see her reaction, she was beginning to turn back to normal, but there was still an air of defense about her– like she was on edge. It made that tiny amount of guilt bury itself deep inside him and remind him that she couldn't have known better. He was mad at her for no real reason— or at least the reason he was mad wouldn't have made any sense to either of them.

"I didn't know that would happen either."

The clown's meek voice drew his attention and he looked up to see her awkwardly squirm under his gaze. She began to shift from color to color, slowly blotching from red to orange to yellow, green, purple while she desperately searched for something better to say.

"I'll find a way to make it up to you.."

She wrung the tails of her hat in her hands nervously, pulling it just hard enough that he caught a glimpse of the bright teal curls underneath it.

"It's fine. It doesn't matter anymore." Oliver rejected, electing to turn away from her and begin cleaning up the uneaten food she had been carrying for nearly two days without his knowledge.

Dindet dropped her hands back to her side in submission and stared at him for a moment, deciding the better option would be to let him alone.

So she left, quietly fading from this world into the liminal place she liked to hide when no one wanted her around. She felt something so small, gnawing at her insides. That it served as a better distraction than being in the same vicinity as someone who, at the moment, clearly wanted nothing to do with her. At night she might sate that gnawing, and probably help the scientist with his machine.

Oliver knew he caused the alien to run off, though he didn't know if she could still see him, or worse, see how he felt about it.

Honestly, to him, he wanted so badly not to care at all. He didn't. Shouldn't. He needed her though, needed to blame her for everything wrong in his life so he could wallow in the slow despair bed he had made for himself and shove all consequence onto her.

Of course, people don't work that way, and he, like everyone else, was an emotional little creature that desired so terribly to lock away all that nonsense and pretend it didn't even exist. She just happened to be the monster that showed up and made sure you knew exactly how awful everything was all the time.

One of the many, many reasons he wanted her out of his life, but also one of the many, many reasons he also kind of, sort of...didn't.

After mopping up the last of the milk, and pulling the quilt out of the wash, Oliver relegated himself to the couch to distract himself with poorly thought out plotlines on TNT schlock detective shows. More intent on numbing his mind with duplicitous buddy cop television than the overwhelming regret he felt about yelling at someone for being completely unconscious.

Peace Zone

It could have been a couple seconds here, or perhaps a few hours not here, by the time Dindet began to mull over some kind of way to amend the situation.

There were many places she could take him, one where you could make the world yourself, there were some that were simple, some that were complex..but she knew of one that would be absolutely perfect.

Of course, she would have to make some minor adjustments.

"Oliver?" The clown appeared on the back of the couch next to him in an instant, causing him to toss the bag of chips he'd been snacking on in shock. The boy shook the startle from his face and eyed her with incredulity.

"Wow, nothing really lasts for you, does it?" He mocked, instantly regretting it as he shifted positions. "Sorry.."

She rolled down from the back of the couch to sit next to him, looking particularly excited, like she was scheming.

"What do you want?" Oliver narrowed his eyes and sighed, already more than reluctant to engage with her.

She should be mad at me still— honestly.

"I know I made you mad earlier and I promised to make it up and I have this place we can go." Dindet began, kicking her feet in quiet excitement.

"The Nursery?"

"No, silly, it's much more fun— they have shops and games and tons of stuff to do and most everyone is nice too!" She beamed at her own description. *Is this some kind of carnival universe or something?*

"What's it called?" Oliver looked back at the television, then toward the slowly fading light in the sky. Hopefully, this place was like her 'In Between', he still had to work on the group project.

Dindet grabbed his hand, forcing his attention back toward her as she yanked him off the couch in a quick, ecstatic, little twirl.

"Oh my gosh! You're gonna love it so much! It's called the Peace Zone, but you can't go looking like *that*!" She stopped him mid-spin to gesture broadly at his general appearance.

"What's wrong with how I look?" he argued, only a little hurt by the comment.

"Well, for starters." The clown created a paintbrush in her hand and slathered him egg white, just about as pale as herself before completing the look with an oversized tie and pants paired with a rainbow wig. "Humans aren't supposed to go through dimensions, so you need to not look like a person."

Dindet framed him in her fingers and giggled in amusement while he recovered from the sudden whiplash she'd provided via vortex costume change.

"Is this really necessary?" He twisted in effort to look at himself before moving toward a spare mirror and letting out a disdainful moan.

"Yes, but I promise it will be so much fun!" she answered, quickly wrapping an arm around his neck and pulling him into an entirely new universe. "The last time I was here, I got to play on—"

Dindet froze, and for a split second turned an uncomfortable blotchy orange before quickly and forcefully twisting her companion away from the wanted poster with her undeniable visage.

Oliver though was more preoccupied with the state of this supposed 'Peace Zone' over the clown.

It was like a mishmash of a fantasy world and a hyper futuristic one, that happened to have an ocean for a sky and trees that grew upside down into what looked like glass floors.

It didn't have any of the same appeal Dindet had hyped it up to be. But was confounding enough on its own, that he was more than satisfied with the result.

Dindet too, was disillusioned by the state of the place— or rather her unwelcomeness in it and quickly, casually, began to twist her appearance just enough that she only somewhat resembled herself.

She pulled off her hat and tucked it quietly into a pocket she'd created as they meandered through dirt road shops on the outskirts of broken spaceships that jutted out of the ground around a giant Coliseum-looking monument.

"Oh my god, you have hair?" Oliver had to do a double-take when he first noticed, it was bright teal and almost completely molded to fit the hat she wore- until it promptly exploded into wiley and unruly curls that he half mindedly shoved his hand into to inspect. It felt like a doll's hair.

"Uh...Yeah?" Dindet gingerly pulled his hand away from the tufts of curls and proceeded to tie it back as best she could.

"Then why do you wear that all the time?" Oliver glanced at the jester hat she had folded neatly in a pocket of overalls that he didn't realize she had decided to create.

The clown pushed the hat slightly further into the pocket.

"It was a gift," she answered casually, as she finished up a few leftover changes to her appearance.

Oliver nodded in quiet understanding before changing the subject.

"How do you know about these places?" he asked, instinctively ducking as a low flying whale groaned loudly overhead.

"I think...I came here with... a friend?" she answered, veering off to the left and down toward a dark alleyway that really only looked like it would bring trouble.

"I've...I've never seen..you with anyone?" Oliver panted, drawing slightly closer in effort to stay as far away as possible from the giant sea urchins that clung to the alley walls.

"They don't exist anymore...not in the same way." Dindet paused, briefly pointing from one direction towards another while she debated on whether or not she was actually going the right way. "I don't think so, at least."

The clown decided on a path that led through what looked like a park, except colorful, giant red plants and pods erupted when she passed them, causing them to open up and puff out a powder of orange spores.

"How long had you been looking for me?" He coughed, swatting his hand in the air in effort to waft away the perfumed spray, suddenly feeling quite lightheaded, and also really, *really* good. Like every synapse in his brain fired off ten times faster.

"I think it's this way..." she mumbled to herself before making a split second ninety-degree turn to the right. "Uhm..somewhere in between two hours and 13.8 billion years?"

Wait, what?

Oliver jerked his head up at the answer, shaking away the traces of plant-induced euphoria.

That didn't really make sense at all.

Granted, time and relative space were concepts entirely unfamiliar to him, so he let the whole thing roll off his shoulder.

Dindet came to a screeching halt, and Oliver unwittingly slammed into her, almost pushing completely through her viscous body.

"Here we are!"

The establishment was some mix of a very traditional-looking UFO that had crashed into a medieval type tavern, causing the entire thing to be surrounded in crystallized shards of sand and rocks which reflected fractal images of them as they passed.

"They won't know I'm not—"

"Don't worry, as long as people think you're a clown, no one will come after you," She interrupted with a comforting smile. And as long as she didn't look like herself, they wouldn't find her.

She casually walked up to what looked like a bar and sat down on a large sunflower that acted as a stool.

"Wo nak I ple oy?" A large green goblin-looking thing turned around with a tankard in his hand, curiously eyeing Dindet as she smiled at him, not answering in the slightest.

"Soy snlowc er la eth mas." He grumbled in reluctance, slamming his hand down on the bar top for her to take.

She obliged and the two quietly had a conversation that may or may not have made Oliver keenly aware of his otherness to this universe.

It was the first he saw with actual other people— well, they looked more like monsters and aliens, and the occasional floating disembodied orb. They were all intelligent though, and knew far more about...well, just about everything than he ever would in his entire lifespan.

And here he was, the alien to this world, trying to figure out whatever customs and culture existed here that Dindet knew about, but he didn't.

"You speak a human language." The goblin looked directly at Oliver, making his skin crawl with his yellow gaze. "Heard you talking to stripes here when yous came in."

Dindet pulled her hand away from their telepathic chat for a moment with a slightly nervous laugh.

"They are the tastiest, you know? So full of so many different feelings. You pick it up after a while," she answered, allowing Oliver the time he desperately needed to save face.

The goblin's black pupils flickered from him to Dindet and back.

"Yous guys looking for food or something?" He eyed Oliver again.

"No, just something fun to do." Dindet cocked her head, reaching out for Oliver's hand in what he thought was an effort to relay some small message.

"Right. Follow me." The goblin set one last glass on the counter before directing the two of them toward a back door.

"Dindet, are you sure we can trust them?" Oliver shrunk further and further behind her as she continued onward. Whatever message she may have meant to send was entirely blocked out by incredibly loud static. She was trying not to show how anxious he was and he knew it.

He also knew that if she did, it would immediately give him away.

The goblin held the door open as the two entered into another alleyway, this one with much fewer urchins and many more shadows that Oliver took notice of immediately.

"You say yous not looking for food but you were trying awful hard not to gobble up my thoughts." The giant goblin stepped in front of the door leading back inside the tavern. "I think you're bigger than you let on, stripes."

Dindet took a hesitant step backward, placing herself deliberately in front of Oliver as the goblin approached.

"I think we have the perfect fun thing for yous to partake in."

Dindet glowered at the goblin, almost backing Oliver against the wall with her slow, defensive steps.

Honestly, the boy thought it was a miracle that she was still not turning different colors in some weird attempt to intimidate this other monster.

"Ow!" Oliver gasped at the tiny shock, jerking up to see that they had been surrounded on all sides, and his only means of protection was frozen solid. Again.

"Pretty smart to turn organic." The goblin casually lifted the angry clown statue over his shoulder like a simple log and smirked at Oliver, just as some faceless henchmen came into view, snatching him up in something akin to a burlap sack that felt more like a bag made of stretchy skin.

"Not smart enough."

***

A small grey alien with large black eyes tossed Oliver out of the skin bag into some dungeon-esque cell with a giant wooden door at the other end.

"Hey! What's the deal?! We didn't do anything!" He scrambled toward the bars as another creature dressed rather flamboyantly came around the corner, carting a large glass jar with what he could only imagine to be Dindet.

"You know, the only thing I hate about your kind is how hard it is to catch you." The androgynous alien flicked its tongue with a smirk. "Of course once you find out someone's weakness it becomes a lot easier."

Oliver glared at the alien as they dollied the jar of real clown into the cell.

"Let- let us out of here!" *Wow, as if that would work.*

Oliver quickly moved to steal away the vulnerable jar from the grasp of this new enemy.

The lizard-like creature blinked its four eyes, two at a time before smiling slyly.

"Oh, you're not in trouble. We just couldn't pass up the opportunity— when Gortho told us two hungry clowns were in the Peace Zone we simply had to take advantage! You *do* make the best entertainment." The alien clapped their hands together in excitement. "It's a win-win!"

Oliver maintained a blazing glare at the creature as it left him to sit in this cold, damp, and dark cell, wrapped around a glass jar full of the only thing he knew that could even potentially fix this—and she was entirely incapacitated.

How stupid could I be?! Thinking that this dumb clown wouldn't screw up everything even worse than before. All of this is because she felt bad and she went ahead and made it ten times worse than it needed to be. She tried to protect me though.

The quiet of the cell did not last very long, as the sound of uproarious cheers and calls echoed softly from outside of the giant door, pulling Oliver deeper into his slow descent into panic and causing his entire body to shake with terrified adrenaline. The large wooden door began to lift, allowing the roaring crowd to penetrate the cells and echo off the stone. He nervously checked the jar, Dindet was slowly returning from a gas to that goopy thing she was before she looked mostly normal.

It was a Coliseum, stacked high with an enormous crowd that cheered as some awful creature was carted away and a giant, humanoid, rock man stood triumphantly with his fist in the air.

"THANK YOU RODER FOR THAT BRILLIANT SHOW!!" A loud voice boomed over a call box at the centermost point of the stands, "AND NOW A MESSAGE FROM OUR SPONSORS, ARE YOU HAVING TROUBLE GETTING YOUR INTERDIMENSIONAL EMAIL TO WORK? GETTING TOO MUCH SPAM AND NOT ENOUGH CLORBECKS? TRY RANDY'S DEMENSITECH! ALL YOUR SOFTWARE NEEDS WITHOUT THE NEED TO MOVE YOUR FEET!"

Oliver stared out at the arena, clutching the jar close to his chest as he hesitantly stepped forth, but not out of the shadows entirely. On the other end of the arena was another door, just as large as this one, and it too was being slowly cranked open to reveal something he would surely dread.

By now, the jar Dindet was residing inside began to crack with the pressure of her as she attempted to escape, forcing Oliver to throw it out of his hands onto the ground to allow the alien to finally regain consciousness.

"What's going on?!" She stammered, twisting around in effort to find her friend. Upon sight, she immediately grabbed his shoulders, checking to see if he was okay and unhurt as his eyes began to widen with sheer terror.

"Oliver, I'm so sorry, I didn't mean for this to happen, I'll get us out of here, I—"

A giant paw landed next to the two of them, and she froze, pulling him close in a hug to shield the fleshy boy from whatever monstrosity growled from behind them.

"OOH, PREEMPTIVE STRIKE! ALL IS WELL THOUGH." The loudspeaker drew the clown's attention and she turned to see what hellish creature stood in the same place as them. "WELCOME BACK TO THE 7,427TH ANNUAL FIGHT ZONE! IT'S NOT EVERY DAY WE GET TO SEE THE EVER-ELUSIVE CLOWNS, BUT DO WE HAVE A TREAT FOR YOU! TWO FEISTY LITTLE BUGGERS FROM THE CORNUCOPIA FOR YOUR ENTERTAINMENT! BE SURE TO CHEER AND CHEER HARD CAUSE THESE LITTLE GUYS LIVE FOR IT— LITERALLY!"

What?

Dindet glanced around, finally and actually taking in her surroundings as the slow realization dawned on her.

Another paw swatted at her, forcing her to dodge with Oliver numbly clinging onto her waist.

"WITHOUT FURTHER ADO, LET THE GAME BEGIN! Sponsored by Randy's Dimensitech."

Dindet ripped Oliver free from herself, taking just a tiny moment to see where the paws were coming from before attempting to escape this universe entirely.

A giant catlike creature stood at the other end of the arena, swatting angrily at trainers as it furiously fanned its colorful feathered tail and flicked its six ears in irritation.

Not worth staying, that was for sure.

The clown grabbed Oliver's hand and made a break for it, trying to get as far out of reach as possible before tumbling headfirst into the ground in a muddled attempt to escape.

"What's wrong?!" Oliver gasped as he pulled air back into his lungs. He frantically glanced from the creature to Dindet, who wore all her worry on her face as she repeatedly tried and failed to manipulate her rate of molecular vibration.

"OOH, THAT HAD TO HURT. NO TRAVELING FOR THESE BEANIE BABIES THOUGH! PATENTED ANTI-MAGNETIC PULSATORS. Brought to you by Randy's Dimensitech."

Dindet spun around, catching sight of the thing which prevented their escape— *how she didn't notice before, she was being so..so careless!*

Giant ringed coils towered at every corner of the arena, giving off an undeniable electromagnetic pulse that was just irregular enough that she and any other clown around her would not be able to leave through dimensional drift.

"I have to win." She spoke softly, almost reluctantly. Not as though she was worried she would lose but more like she was worried about breaking something in the process, or worse. Losing control.

"You can't! That— that thing is huge! I— we have to get out of here!" Oliver grappled with words, still jittery from the fight or flight response his body refused to let go of.

Dindet offered a comforting smile before pushing him against the wall.

"I'm bigger."

The clown stepped in front of him and held a hand out as some meager guard against attack before putting her fingers to her lips to sound off a near ear-piercing whistle.

Oliver cupped his ears and clenched his eyes shut at the growls from the cat beast as its attention drew to them.

The animal– if it was that— was enormous, colorful, and clearly very angry at whatever caused it to be stuck here.

"HEY!" Dindet called, whistling once more to gather all of its attention.

Why?? You're leading it right to us! Stop!

The creature howled, swatting away the few trainers left before charging directly at the two of them, forcing Oliver to put every last bit of trust he had into the only thing between him and certain death.

The ground shook with each step, and he couldn't help but flinch in anticipation. It wasn't until he heard uproarious..laughter?

He peeked, searching the area to see what exactly happened.

The beast had stopped dead in its tracks, bobbing its head as it followed a giant ball of yarn that was surely the clown as she weaved around its legs, causing the thing to rear up on its haunches and confusedly chase her.

She was forcing it back, bouncing all over the place and letting it bat at her until she was completely launched into the air, at which point she spun furiously before turning back into herself and revealing a far too oversized mallet that she brought down hard onto the top of its head.

The impact of the two left a crater of considerable size, and the cat monster hissed loudly in frustration, writhing and twisting out of the crater in effort to find its pest.

"LOOKS LIKE THINGS ARE GETTING CATTY BETWEEN THESE TWO!" The announcer cheered, distracting the clown for a split second too long and allowing the cat beast to swipe, tossing her into the air and clawing her back down with a thud. The beast began to seethe until its giant, pupil-less green eyes caught sight of Oliver crouching by the door.

It launched itself forward, and in an instant, Dindet appeared in front of him, only to be completely eviscerated by the creature's claws.

The crowd hushed, and Oliver hastily wiped the remains of her from his face to see.

The cat creature licked its saber teeth, preparing to pounce just as the starry slime it had spewed everywhere began to bubble and churn.

Long tentacles shot out from the puddles, converging as the galactic entity reformed into something that Oliver had never once seen.

Its glowing white eyes peered down at the creature, dwarfing it in comparison to its sheer size. Suddenly a horrific, metallic shriek erupted from it, like millions of voices all at once, and the mere animal cowered, bristling up as it backed away.

One, then another clawed limb landed in the dirt, digging large crevices into it as what was at one point Dindet prepared to launch itself toward the prey. But it didn't.

Instead, the nightmare creature melted, letting out one last horrific screech before it collapsed into nothing and the familiar face of the clown stared back at her friend.

"Oliver, I'm so sorry."

Only Just a Little

"I can't believe you did that!" Oliver tore off his colorful wig as the two reappeared in the living room covered in whatever that universe considered decorative flowers.

"I'm really sorry, I should have visited to make sure it was okay to go before—"

"Are you kidding me?!" Oliver cut her off, letting out an enthusiastic sigh of laughter as he moved toward the kitchen for a spare towel. "You were so freaking cool! I thought we were gonna die— *literally*– and you just— shwoOMPH!"

The boy mimicked the way she grew with a gesture of his arms, "you got huge! And we won! The *championship*! It was the coolest thing I've ever seen!"

The clown stared at him in utter bafflement, more prepared for scolding than praise. It was dumb of her to risk either of them like that and she was sure he would be mad at her for it, or maybe the adrenaline hadn't quite worn off yet.

"You're not mad?" She questioned, setting the prizes they had won down on the coffee table.

"Well, I'm pretty sure I should be traumatized— but that was just, like– the most awesome thing I've ever seen. And also I think these flowers might be some kind of drug? Because I'm feeling *pretty* good." Oliver rubbed the paint off his face with a wet towel and jumped back onto the couch to review all the weird things they had won from the tournament.

Some weird red flowers that exploded glowing orange spores that he was sure were what alleviated the majority of his jitters, a gift certificate to Randy's Dimensitech Outpost, and a crystalline medal with their names etched onto the surface.

"We have to do that again." He mused, sorting out the prizes to admire.

Dindet stared at them for a moment, more consumed by other far more dangerous things than fighting a Vodnys.

She wouldn't say anything about it.

"What time.." Oliver reached to his left to grab the clock, not even two minutes had passed here, and they had spent what– at least four hours in that other universe? "We weren't even gone for five minutes!"

What he didn't realize though, was that regardless of how long they were gone from here, there was still a severe jet lag that would inevitably hit him like a rock the second he sat down for more than a couple minutes. And it did.

He was knocked out only after three minutes into a bad sci-fi movie, head thrown back over the couch and gurgling with each snore.

***

Oliver jumped, startling himself awake from the remnants of a nightmare, and peered around the dark room. At least three hours had passed since he'd dozed off, as the sun had already set and a very light snow was cascading down outside.

The boy shifted, cracking his neck and taking a brief moment to massage the tender spot where it bent on the back of the couch before getting up to head to his room.

He could faintly hear the clacking of his father working on the machine upstairs and figured the clown was helping him, so he meandered into the kitchen to grab a glass of water to take with him.

As he turned back, he froze, a split second of terror jolting through him before he realized that the dark silhouette sitting outside on the porch was Dindet.

Why is she like that? She doesn't have to stay outside all night.

Quietly, he slid the door open to check on her- just to see if she was frozen like last time.

She wasn't, at least not yet, though a thin film of frost grew at the edges of her and she was lightly powdered in snow.

"You don't have to stay outside all night, you know?" He broke the silence, causing her to glance back at him before nodding slowly.

"I know, I just like to," she answered softly, placing a hand on Egg who sat in her lap.

Oliver hesitated, focusing a little too long on the cat as he tried to come up with something to say next, but his brain was going all sorts of slow.

"You're not cold?"

"No."

She should be though, considering she is covered in frost and snow, and judging by the breeze, it'll only get colder.

"Do..." Oliver glanced back inside the house for a moment, "do you want some hot cocoa?"

Dindet tilted her head, looking back at him.

"I don't know what that is," she answered plainly, almost like she was only half here and the other half was somewhere else.

Oliver nodded to himself, a gentle reminder that, of course, she wouldn't know what hot cocoa was. "It's a drink, I'll be right back."

He gestured for her to stay put and ran back inside to work on two large cups of cocoa, the one thing he was most confident in making and if she had any taste buds, he was sure she would love it.

On the way back, he grabbed the quilt from the dryer and wrapped it around his shoulders like an oversized cape before sliding the door open, holding out the cup for the clown to take.

Dindet obliged, and watched him sit criss-cross next to her, piling up a still hot quilt around himself and setting his own cup in between his legs.

"You drink it. But..please do something with it if you don't have a stomach." Oliver took a sip from his mug and watched her, waiting for her to mimic him. "Is it good?"

Dindet lowered her cup and cocked her head in mild confusion. "I don't know."

Oh...

"What is it supposed to taste like?" she asked, taking another sip as if to please him. Oliver looked down at his drink, watching the steam of it rise and swirl in the cold night air while he pieced together all the different flavors.

"It's warm..and creamy? I used vanilla creamer and milk instead of water. And I put a little bit of peppermint in it too, so kind of minty, and then chocolate powder, so that's sweet," he explained as best he could, though he didn't think it mattered all that much in the long run.

"Oh, like kindness?" Dindet looked at the cup and took another, much bigger swig.

"Uh, I guess so?" If that was what she could relate it to, then he figured it worked just as well.

There was a silence between them, for long enough to make Oliver slightly uncomfortable.

"My mom and I used to do this," he said, regretting it immediately, "She liked to look at the stars."

He glanced up at the night sky, it was cloudy, the only light came trickling out behind clouds that drifted over the moon and made the snow look like stars in the place of the real ones.

"Do you miss your friend?" He changed the subject, blinking away spare tears before glancing back at the clown and her silly hat. She nodded, deftly pulling on a tail as she lowered her gaze.

"You get really quiet when you're upset." Oliver mentioned, "I noticed that."

"I don't think you're very good at being a clown."

There was another silence that drifted over them, one that he didn't want to tread on. The alien was something he didn't quite comprehend. It was like she was here and also not.

Some cosmic weird thing that only ever half existed. He wondered if she liked it here. If she liked being around him.

Probably not.

But he was starting to like being around her.

***

Oliver stood in his room, reading and re-reading the court order over and over again. It was late now, and he probably should have gone to bed. But a creeping anxiety built up in his chest, making him shake and tremble every few seconds.

He didn't tell his dad about it when it came, and he wasn't entirely sure why. Maybe because it was inevitable. Or because he knew deep down that he deserved it.

Oliver folded up the piece of paper and moved to his door, really and truly contemplating whether or not he should bring it up. If he could make it stop.

The house was dark, aside from the buzzing light that emanated from the crack below the attic door. His dad was up still, working on his machine with the blueprints Dindet had drawn out for him.

The project was going to take a lot longer now.

Oliver crept across the balcony, and quietly opened the door for a peek. His step-father lay on the floor, rewiring some electrical component on the left of the machine. The bright spotlight he had on cascaded the room in a bluish glow that made him look more pale than he actually was.

"...Dad?" Oliver said softly, pushing the door open a little, just until it scraped against one of the mouse cages on the floor.

Jon grunted and pushed himself backward, wedging his torso between the table and the machine in effort to get a better look at the wiring he was working with. But he didn't answer.

"Dad," Oliver repeated, this time prompting the man to crane his neck out to look at him.

"Hey Ols, what's up? It's a school night, you should be asleep by now."

The boy retreated slightly, still in the process of deciding to tell his father about the letter.

"I couldn't sleep, and I wanted to know how...how much longer before it's done." He lied, hiding the paper in his hand behind the door.

Jon made another noise and thrust himself out from under the machine, stumbling to his feet as he got up to face his son.

"Well." He rubbed his neck. "Dindet was kind enough to inform me that all my calculations are incorrect, and I've killed about twenty mice."

"So I have to start from scratch, and that'll probably take me about six more months."

Oliver kept his eyes on the floor. *That's way too long. The letter came in August. If we don't get her back before—*

"Luckily, our alien friend can either find or make all the parts I need," Jon interrupted his thoughts, "so it's probably gonna be closer to two or three more months. I'm betting we'll be finished before winter break."

"What if something happens?" It was innocuous enough. Oliver kept his eyes on the floor though. "Before then, I mean."

His father gave pause, pressing his thumb to his chin in a

moment of thought before he knelt down in front of the boy and set his hand on his shoulder. "I've got everything worked out, Dindet is in the system as an exchange student remember? No one knows she's an alien. Not even the lab."

That's not what I meant.

"I made sure to get copies of the paperwork, and forge the necessary signatures too," Jon continued, oblivious to his child's growing unease. "So even if something did happen, I have all the legal documents in order."

"That's good," Oliver answered hollowly, enough that Jon took notice and cocked his head in confusion.

"Is there anything you've been worried about?" he asked softly, "you know you can talk to me about it, I promise I won't be mad."

Now would have been a really good time to say something. Perfect, in fact. But Oliver instead shook his head.

He was wrong. He would be mad. I waited so long to say something, that if he did now, it would just make things worse.

All Dad really cares about was that machine. Getting Mom back.

I just get in the way.

"No, that's all I was worried about."*All he wants is his wife back, right? He probably doesn't actually want just...me.*

"You're sure?" Jon questioned gently. Oliver quietly and discreetly tucked the letter into his pocket and nodded.

"You got a lot of stuff to do, sorry I bothered you." The kid drew back from his dad and stepped toward the doorway with a fake half-smile. "I'm gonna head to bed."

"Wait, you didn't—" Jon reached out, attempting to bring himself to his feet before his son shut the attic door. "bother me.."

Shot Through the Heart

"**D**indet!" Douglass was halfway down the road the moment he began sprinting hard to meet up with the two of them as they kicked through a few inches of snow to get off the front porch.

He caught up with them, almost slipping over the melted and packed ice as he dragged in quick and cold breaths.

"I'm so sorry about the other day, I didn't know you would get hurt, I swear!" He tugged lightly on the clown's hand, causing her to blankly stare at him.

"Oh, uh, it's really okay." She offered a smile, taking back her hand in effort to get the very uncomfortable taste of regret out of her mouth. "You wouldn't have known, so it's fine."

Douglass circled her as the three of them made the trek to the bus stop, profusely apologizing to her as though her response simply wasn't enough.

"Dude, she said it's fine," Oliver remarked, finally getting the boy to quiet down, or really get him to talk about some other subject.

"Oh, did you guys finish the project?" Douglass pulled out his phone and began flipping through messages from Cassidy, "Cas wants your part of the analysis so she can finish editing the paper, I finished with the poster, but I wanted to ask if maybe you could do some art for it?"

Oliver begrudgingly nodded, "I'll give her my paper at school."

He hadn't even written his paper, so that's the best he could have offered. Granted, two of the three days he had to work on it were spent running around alternate dimensions, and honestly, he preferred that to homework on all fronts.

The three of them filed into the bus and Douglass moved to sit next to Oliver as opposed to Dindet in not very much effort to remain discrete.

"So, it really isn't a big deal?" He spoke softly, his eyes flickering back to the rather oblivious alien behind him. "I feel really bad, cause my dad said that it wasn't supposed to be a strong enough current to do anything, she isn't mad at me is she? She looks mad."

"She's not mad." Oliver rolled his eyes and scooted as far from the boy as he could manage, only to have Douglass lean in closer.

"You swear, right? I mean— I might have ruined my chance!"

You don't have a chance Douglass, she's not a human person.

"Why do you care so much?" Oliver pressed himself up against the cold metal of the bus, "She hasn't even done anything to prove that you even have a chance."

"Well, I mean, neither have you?"

WHAT?

Oliver sputtered, struggling to find a comeback as the kid went on nonchalantly.

"Yeah, but I have this plan, and I know that if I try hard enough and do all the right things then she'll absolutely fall in love." Douglass continued, ignoring the baffled look he got from Oliver.

What sort of delusion did this poor kid have that made him believe that an alien blob shaped like a girl would fall for cheesy romantic tropes? Or any girl for that matter?

He must have severely misinterpreted the opportunity he thought he had in getting the both of them away from him. All he did was wrap himself up in stupid crush nonsense that he knew, without a single doubt in his head, wouldn't work.

"Douglass, look, I know you think this..plan or whatever is going to work but trust me, she's not like regular girls."

"I know!" Douglass nodded enthusiastically, bobbing up to catch a heartfelt glance at Dindet. "That's why I wanna try!"

This is a waste of time.

"You don't..ugh.." Oliver let out a reluctant sigh and pressed his fingers to the bridge of his nose in effort to calm the last couple of nerves Douglass was fraying. "Fine. Do your dumb plan. But don't come crying to me when it blows up in your face."

Douglass did a brief and frankly, stupid looking little wiggle of excitement and reached into his backpack to pull out a notebook and share this 'plan' of his.

"Okay, so I had to rework it a little after I messed up with Dad's electro-doohickey, but! I have the perfect way to fix it." Douglass flipped his notebook to a page filled with too many doodles and a list of cheesy date options. "First, I can use this one as an apology, and also give a little tour around the old part of town— you know, Pearl Park and the tourist district? Then, she'll forgive me for real and I can follow up with a dinner date Sunday night, right?"

Douglass glanced at Oliver enthusiastically, to which he provided a more than fake smile.

"Then, after a really romantic dinner, I'll take her down to the lake to watch the sunset and we'll kiss, and it'll be perfect!"

About as perfect as a cliche romance that Oliver imagined would end in terrible tragedy. Though, a more vindictive part of him wanted to watch the whole thing unfold, despite how it made him cringe.

"Sounds great," he muttered, getting up the second the bus screeched to a halt in an effort to push Douglass out of his way, and escape this seemingly perpetual one-sided conversation.

Dindet trailed slightly behind the two of them as they hopped off the bus and made their way toward what she knew to be the cafeteria, the place that most human beings went to eat.

"Boys are like that." The familiar voice made her turn toward Cassidy. She casually walked up beside her. "They only like to hang around us because we do all the work for them. So, how do you like it so far?"

The clown stared at her, not quite getting what she meant.

"When I first moved here, nobody talked to me at all, and I have always had a really hard time making friends— so I know you probably feel the same." Cassidy pulled large chunks of her coiled hair into a bun and tied it on the top of her head before gesturing for the clown to follow her to the cafeteria. "And even then, Oliver would be the last person I would want to stay with, even if it was temporary."

At that Dindet hesitated, glancing around to see where he had gone.

"What do you mean?" she asked, still searching the general area. Cassidy held back a small chuckle, as though it was such an obvious thing.

"Well, he's not very nice. I mean, I understand why, but in my opinion, it doesn't matter. You should still always be kind, you know?" The girl lead Dindet to a table and sat down with a couple of other also girls, one that was enthusiastically scarfing down a poorly made omelet and another who had a compact mirror held close to her face while she wiped black gunk on her eyelashes with incredible focus.

"I don't think he's not nice?" Dindet argued rather meekly, recalling the hot cocoa that was supposed to be like kindness he had given to her.

"I mean—" Cassidy began to backtrack, "he used to be so different, like, really quiet. But not, you know, a jerk about it."

"You're that weird girl living with the kid whose mom died, aren't you? Did you know he used to be a girl?" The girl with gunk on her eyes piped up, snapping shut her toy and eyeing Dindet inquisitively, blatantly ignoring the glare Cassidy gave her as she spoke.

"Does he like, cry at night? I heard his dad went crazy and that's why you're here. Theo said his mom offed hersel—"

"Hailey!" Cassidy chided, placing a protective hand on Dindet's shoulder.

"What? Why else would he like, adopt a whole kid if it wasn't to fill some hole or whatever?" She casually remarked, "it's not like she wouldn't know. So, is it true that he almost died?"

The girl finished whatever strange primping she was doing and shoved the tools she used back into her bag before standing up and rounding the two of them, not waiting for an answer.

"Honestly Cas, why'd you bring her over here? Is she like your new project or something? Cause *wow*." Hailey let out a sarcastic laugh, "you got your work cut out for you."

Cassidy made a judicious face at the girl as she left before turning back to the clown with an empathetic smile.

"I'm really sorry about her, she's really not as brutal as she comes off." The girl beckoned for Dindet to sit down next to her and the other girl who had successfully foundered herself on reconstituted egg. "So, where are you from? I was born in Senegal, and moved here when I was ten."

"I..uh." without Oliver around, Dindet struggled to find a plausible answer. "I'm from the Cornucopia."

Cassidy cocked her head as if she were listing off countries and states in her mind that she knew to exist.

"I've never heard of that place before, is it new?" she questioned, cornering the alien into her lie. Dindet held back her quiet panic, glancing every which way while she desperately searched for the only human in this place she could trust.

"I- uh, it's-"

"What are you doing?"

Sweet relief. It almost made her jump. Oliver spoke quizzically from over her shoulder. The clown dipped down and quickly scrambled out of her chair, shrinking back behind him.

"Cassidy was asking me about where I'm from is all."

Oliver eyed the two girls dubiously.

"It's a remote town in the Netherlands." He lied, catching Dindet ever so slightly chameleon into a calmer state. She nodded briskly and wrapped his hand in hers as a quiet 'thank you'.

"Huh, I'll have to ask my mom about it sometime," Cassidy replied, only half believing them. "Well, I guess I'll see you in class."

The boy's eyes narrowed. There was a tone in her voice that Oliver quickly gathered as an 'I'm watching you'.

"See you," he gruffly responded, already on his way out with Dindet chasing behind him.

Cassidy got on his nerves only a little less than Douglass, who was mostly just annoying. Cassidy, on the other hand, was the type of person who pitied you.

Oliver knew it, and so did just about everyone in school.

She had a habit of collecting kids that she believed needed to be fixed or helped in some way and coddled them like she was trying to be their mother. Most everyone caught on after the first couple of years though, so now she targeted new kids and kept them in her circle. He knew exactly what she was trying to do.

"You have to be more careful, or else people are gonna catch on. Especially when you—" *start changing colors? Don't say that, it'll just make it worse.* "You need to learn how to lie better."

Dindet stayed fairly quiet as she followed behind Oliver while he ranted on about maintaining the illusion that she was a human being. Her thoughts on the matter were close to nil, as she was preoccupied with what Cassidy had said to her earlier.

"Are you a nice person?"

Oliver stopped mid-rant, genuinely shocked at the question.

"Well..that's subjective," he muttered, turning to face away from her, "that's like asking if someone's a good person."

"Are you?" Dindet questioned, quickening her pace to catch up.

"Well, I...I like to think I am?" *I'm not.* "It's a matter of what you and– and what other people think, I think?"

Eight in the morning was definitely not the best of times to be mulling over moral philosophy with a creature that had no idea what it was, while also being far too under-educated on the matter himself.

"It's more like, well, I think it's more like what you try to do versus what actually happens?" The boy gestured awkwardly at nothing as if waving a hand in the air would somehow make it gain any semblance of sense. "Like all you are is what you do and how you and other people think of it? I don't know, why do you even care?"

"Cassidy said you're not a nice person and I wanted to know if it was true."

"She doesn't know me," Oliver answered, dropping his gaze to the floor and dropping the conversation altogether.

He ruminated on the idea for the entirety of the morning, taking quick glances back at the girl as she chit-chatted with the clown in between classes, and helped her with schoolwork.

"Hey, do you need any help with that?" He twisted around in his chair to face the alien, all while watching Cassidy curl up in shock at the mere fact he'd spoken.

Dindet glanced from the girl, back to Oliver with more than a little confusion, silently wondering why he was all of the sudden so interested.

"I know English is hard for you, and this page has a lot of

writing too." He reached over and pressed a finger down on her paper, pointing out the large paragraph question she would eventually have to answer.

This was not something she was used to, majority of the time Oliver only ever helped her when school was over and they were at home.

Usually, at this place, he wanted nothing to do with anyone and reeked of general boredom, disgust, and a strong twang of anxiety. Which she gathered to be how he felt most of the time about school and all the people inside it.

"Oh..okay," the clown nodded slowly, still trying to wrap her head around the sudden change of behavior. "I'd like that, please."

Oliver briskly nodded and stood up, taking the empty seat between the two of them and flipping to the page needed to answer the question, only elbowing Dindet softly when she unknowingly began to turn green with his quiet envy.

"That's really nice of you, Oliver." Cassidy's not-quite-sarcasm made his face burn.

"I help her all the time at home, it's nothing," he answered, not looking at her and instead pointing out the passage for Dindet; who was still battered by the push and pull of the two's emotional hurricane that raged on just beneath the surface.

It was already hard enough hiding in plain sight but this, she imagined, was entirely unnecessary. And entirely unpleasant.

The majority of the morning was this odd mental battle over who was offering the clown the better assistance.

As each kid took their turn, Cassidy offering notes, followed by a retaliation from Oliver offering homework to copy. Over time Dindet grew frustrated at the silly war going on over her head.

"I'm gonna..go somewhere else," she said politely, sliding out from underneath her desk in order to find the only other human she knew that wasn't inconveniencing her with a bombardment of confusing kindness.

She quietly moved into the desk behind Douglass.

"Hey?"Dindet tapped his shoulder to gather his attention.

"H-hey!" The boy twisted around in his seat, turning bright red once he realized who was behind him.

Dindet's eyes flickered back to Oliver and Cassidy as they stopped helping her and started helping each other, if not purely out of spite.

"Can I hang out over here for a bit?" she asked, keeping her voice low enough not to cause any disruptions.

Douglass turned back to see the not-so-subtle war going on in front of him and nodded.

"Having a psychic battle," he said with a small chuckle, leaning back to allow Dindet to hear him without raising his voice. "If you look hard enough, you can see the sparks."

Dindet nodded, not quite getting the joke. Mostly because she *could* see the sparks.

Douglass twisted around in effort to get a better look at her. "Since they are..being dumb, do you wanna maybe, I dunno, like...hang out? I mean like, without them, but if you don't want to-"

"That sounds fun!" the alien replied after a brief moment of weighing the pros and cons of dealing with Oliver's inevitable grumpiness versus Douglass's relatively pleasant infatuation.

The boy looked as though he would physically implode at her answer, and responded with an overtly subdued excitement that Dindet found tasteful despite his effort to hide it.

"Really? Err- uh, cool. That's cool. Cool.." Douglass straightened, and puffed himself up with pseudo confidence, "I'll pick you up after school?"

***

"Oh god, please don't tell me." Oliver smacked his palm to his forehead and let out a beleaguered groan in anticipation of what he knew she would say. "Douglass asked you out?"

The clown nodded, donning the goofiest, stupidest grin he had ever seen, not comprehending the type of 'asking out' she had so eagerly agreed to.

"He said we were gonna go to the park—"

"Bad news," the subject in question interrupted, glancing down at his phone with a disenchanted frown. "My dad said he can't pick us up because of a new thing he's adding to his energy machine."

Douglass lowered his head in shame and shoved his phone back into his pocket. "I guess we can reschedule for some other time, maybe."

Dindet cocked her head, taking in a flavor of sadness that, for once, didn't come from Oliver.

"It's okay," she said, resting an empathetic hand on the boy's shoulder. "We can still..."

She trailed off, watching confoundedly as Oliver gestured silently- albeit frantically from behind Douglass, making a large X with his arms in hopes to get her to stop saying what he knew she was gonna say next.

"We can what?" Douglass stared at her intently while the alien slowly tried to piece together Oliver's horrid pantomime.

"We..can still...go? For a walk?"

Oliver smacked himself in the head in frustration. Why he thought that would work was a mystery, at least she didn't offer a hop and a skip to another world— which would have been considerably worse.

"I mean, we still have time before the bus leaves, you can just—
"

"I know the perfect place!" Douglass interrupted Oliver's last-ditch effort to break the two's plans before very awkwardly placing his arm around the clown's shoulder, which she just as promptly removed. "You can take the bus home if you want, Ols."

Douglass craned his neck back to offer an unsubtle wink to

him as he and the *not-a-human-girl* began down the sidewalk, leaving him standing utterly dumbfounded at the edge of the bus lanes.

***

Dindet kept fairly quiet aside from small 'ooh's and 'aww's at the various locations Douglass proudly pointed out as he led her down a winding path toward South Pearl Park.

"Oh my gosh, what is that!?" She gasped at the sight of something strange and stringy in the distance, making a break for it with an enthusiastic scamper. The clown circled around a large pole that stuck up from the ground with colorful, twinkling lights that attached at the top and splayed out in a cone.

"It's a decoration. The city puts them out every winter," Douglass answered as casually as possible while he tried very, very hard not to squeal with a similar level of excitement at her childish wonder. "They're supposed to look like trees."

"That's so cool! Oliver never told me about these! Or trees!" She giggled, spinning around the pole for a short moment before her attention caught something even more exciting. "What. Is. That."

The clown weaved through the stringed lights and immediately made a B-line for a duck haplessly waddling to a shallow pond.

"You have no teeth," she murmured, crouching down to get the best look she could. She mimicked its waddles as she returned to Douglass and immediately got smacked in the face with the raw stench of his emotions.

The boy rubbed his neck, oozing anxiety with every hesitant opening of his mouth before actually saying what he intended to say.

"I, uh, I wanted to say sorry for hurting you the other day." He began, taking a small step closer to her.

"It's okay, I know you didn't mean to." Dindet nodded and

turned away, attempting to beckon the duck out of the pond and trying her best not to turn yellow.

"I just wanted you to know that I...was." Douglass kept his eyes on the duck as a momentary distraction while he summoned the courage to speak. "Because I really like you."

"I like you too!" Dindet turned around, succeeding in collecting the duck and holding it in her arms. "You're a nice person."

Oof. She missed the point.

Douglass offered a nervous smile as he panicked to find a way to maybe clarify better for her.

"I mean, I..uh, like-like you." He brushed his clammy hands through his curls and watched while the girl walked completely through the concept, past him, and toward a stone bench.

"I..like you too?" She repeated, slightly confused by his poor choice of wording.

Douglass shook his head and followed her, sitting down and petting the duck she held in her lap.

"I think Oliver would—"

"Dindet, I have feelings for you," Douglass interrupted, louder than he intended, but he was sure it got the message across, right?

She stared at him for a moment, then blinked, then smiled softly. *Oh thank god, she understood.*

"Well, yeah, everyone has feelings."

No. No, she didn't.

The boy folded in on himself with a pained sigh, suddenly realizing what his friend actually meant when he said Dindet wasn't like regular girls. *Maybe this calls for an act as opposed to words?*

And luckily there's a universal method of sharing one's feelings. Douglass turned toward the clown and maintained eye contact for as long as he could before leaning in closer, closing his eyes, and puckering his lips.

Only for two hands to firmly sandwich his face and completely halt his efforts.

The boy's eyes opened wide with shock and confusion while Dindet held him curiously between her hands, cocking her head with a look that resembled both extreme discomfort and curiosity. The duck sitting in her lap quacked, breaking the unusual tension and hopping off to waddle back into its pond.

"What are you doing?" She asked, mushing his face a little, somehow expecting a response from him with his cheeks pushed together like a bad fish impression.

"I maswhanna kishu..?" Douglass attempted, then reached up to pull her hands away so he could actually speak. "I..was gonna kiss you?"

"Why?" Her voice was incredulous, almost like she'd never even heard of the universal love gesture.

"I..love you?" Douglass watched with ever-growing regret as her eyes darted away from him and her brow furrowed in further discomfort.

"I'm not...I can't.." Dindet backed away anxiously, trying to find an answer that wouldn't blow her cover. "I don't...do that."

The poor boy looked like he was about to cry, but he smiled nonetheless, burying his regret as far down as he possibly could, unaware that the alien knew exactly where it lay.

Dindet stood up, glancing back and forth as if she expected Oliver to come out of nowhere to provide the alibi she desperately needed to escape Douglass's strengthening sorrow that seeped through the barrier she'd set up and tainted her blue.

"I'm..gonna– I'm gonna go."

***

Oliver lay on the couch, splayed out and flipping from app to app in a tired, useless effort to fend off boredom alongside other swirling thoughts in his head.

It wasn't that he wasn't used to being home essentially alone, all summer his dad spent in the attic, and the silence in the house was common, especially after—

Still though, for the short period of time the clown was around, he had gotten comfortable with her.

She provided the much-needed escape from the drudgery of school, and people, and everything, while also very inconveniently being a constant reminder of why he wanted to escape in the first place. Of course, he forced himself not to care about it, or anything for that matter, least of all an alien clown.

His eyes glazed over with the repeated switching from various social media apps, refreshing each one in a mind-numbing cycle that didn't really serve a purpose until the easily recognizable presence of Dindet caused him to glance over at where she appeared on the other side of the coffee table.

"How did it go?" he asked, focusing back on his phone. The lack of a response prompted him to sit up and actually look at her.

She was very slowly returning from a deep blue shade, looking more than uncomfortable at whatever went down on their little date.

Oliver hesitated, feeling a pang of sympathy for her and almost voicing it too.

"Wasn't what you expected, was it?" He said instead, resituating himself so that if she wanted, she could sit down next to him. The clown obliged and sat down, not speaking nor giving any indication that she wanted to. She looked as though she were thinking incredibly hard about something that didn't make sense to her at all.

"Is everythi—"

"Am I good?" She interrupted, not turning to look at him as she clenched her fists in anticipation.

Oliver opened his mouth, not quite finding the words he probably needed but speaking nonetheless.

"I don't—"

"Because you said to be good, other people have to feel about you, right? And I can tell when they feel bad. And I make a lot of people feel bad..." She rambled, losing some bit of herself to a stress he didn't realize existed.

She looked like she was desperately trying to hold herself together, that just under the surface of what could be considered skin, was a soft boiling that intensified the longer she kept speaking.

"What I meant was that, well, sometimes it—" Oliver struggled, only just noticing how he had backed himself into a corner with his horrid explanations. "What other people think doesn't matter as much as what you think."

"And I—" He paused. "I don't think you're bad."

It was something of a half-truth, really. He didn't think she was an awful person, not at all, maybe a little naive but no monster.

While at the same time, he didn't like her at all for reasons he knew that if he tried to confront, would be shown to be just as preposterous as they were.

"If anything, I'm bad," Oliver said softly.

The clown nodded to herself and mustered up strength enough to push down his growing self-hatred to show off a bright, albeit unconvincing smile.

"I don't think you're bad. I think you're good too, just sad," she said, standing up from the couch and making her way to the edge of the stairs.

The idea was nice but deep down Oliver knew better. If anything, he was cruel- purposefully to her. He wanted to be because it made him feel just a little better.

Though now, regret was forming in his chest, making it a little harder to breathe.

My Other Dad

"Hey, Oliver!" the clown whispered, just loud enough that the boy napping on the couch clenched his eyes shut in silent brace before opening them.

She was just a hair's width from his face, wearing a goofy grin that would have been amusing if it weren't for her immediate closeness startling him up and smacking her hard with his head.

She winced and clapped her hands over her nose, promptly hopping off the couch and dizzily rippling in effort to quell the lingering ache.

"I'm sorry!" Oliver started, moving to console her but she waved him off, squatting down for a moment to let out a stifled groan before spinning around with a slightly forced smile.

"It's okay! It wasn't on purpose!" she rebutted, dismissing the entire thing with a gentle pat of his head.

Oliver followed her as she meandered around the house, picking up and inspecting various things with some level of impunity.

"What are you looking for?" he asked, taking all the things she'd casually thrown on the ground in her search. "Also, please put stuff back where you find it if you don't need it."

Dindet turned heel, almost crashing into him once again and only saving face by becoming a gas that merely phased through him entirely.

"What is that stuff Mr. Your Dad puts in his bowl of wet string?" she asked, glancing around the kitchen in effort to find it.

"Spice?" Oliver questioned.

"Yeah!" She nodded. "I wanna try something I think will be cool."

"With..spice..?" Oliver reaffirmed with a tone more indicative of confusion than anything else. "It's in the cupboard."

What else am I gonna do? If I didn't tell her, odds were she was going to unmake just about everything in the kitchen, remake them, and just leave it all in places that it probably shouldn't be.

He decided that regardless of telling her exactly where it was, he ought to at least keep an eye on the alien. She haplessly clambered up the counter to reach the cupboard, searching for the ingredients she desired to use in a concoction he was only partially concerned the purpose of.

His eyes trailed away from her and toward a pile of mail that hadn't been opened for at least a few months, all stacked on the island. Most of them looked to be letters of condolences, some were just junk and a few looked to be important.

Oliver glanced back at the clown, she didn't seem to be causing or having much trouble, and for once she wasn't just throwing things she didn't want over her shoulder. So he opted to take the small chance and bring the stack of mail up to his father.

Weekends were like this, Jon would work all night with the clown to rebuild his machine the correct way and then sleep all day. So Oliver spent majority of his time either vegetating on the couch long enough to fall asleep without the usual nightmares. Or alternatively, being carted off to some other dimension to babysit an easily distracted clown in effort to get errands that didn't exist here.

Most of the places they went were amusing, different at least. Dindet just had a consistent habit of forgoing necessity in lieu of fun. Which didn't bother him in the slightest.

"Dad, we have a bunch of mail." Oliver pushed the door open, having to force it a little harder than usual due to the excess and frankly, poorly drawn blueprints Dindet had modified that piled up around the entrance.

There was a soft glow in the room, coming from the laptop that had been left open on the table. His father was further back, crookedly splayed out on the old futon with a drool puddle of considerable size right next to his face.

He stirred for a moment, moaning as he turned over and murmured a nothing word.

Oliver briefly went through the letters, majority of it was at least a few months old; a cheap condolence letter from the lab, and a newer one that had a big red URGENT stamp on it, some junk mail for buying crappy timeshares, a funeral catalog, and a couple from the law firm that he casually slid into his pocket and out of sight.

He stacked the rest neatly together and set them next to the laptop, glancing back at his dad once more before quietly backing out and shutting the door.

"What are you trying to do?" Oliver asked, making his way down the stairs to see Dindet with a combination of several colorful spices set out neatly in front of her.

"I think...if I can mix these together the right way and with a little bit of sulfur and potassium nitrate, I can do something really cool," she answered, casually tearing off a small piece of herself to mix in with the ingredients in order to make something entirely new.

She poured the mixture into her hand and balled it up, giving Oliver a cheeky grin before she tossed it into the air.

The little ball of whatever it was she made crackled and

popped, exploding into a miniature firework that dissipated shortly after the embers-but-not-quite began falling. The concoction and little explosion left a fragrant scent in the air, something akin to roasted chicken.

"What was the point of—" Oliver was cut off by a hard and loud knock on the door. He fell quiet for a moment, holding out a hand to gesture for the clown to stay put as he rounded her and made his way to the door.

Guests weren't common, aside from Douglass or his father, but even then, they didn't come around often.

"Yeah–hh.." Oliver stared up at a face he recognized, and a giant gaping hole opened up underneath him and swallowed him whole; already in the process of digesting him in his entirety before he could utter another word.

"Hey, Baby girl."

As immediately as the unbridled terror gripped him, Dindet whipped around to see the cause, turning a deep purple that reflected his fear.

"You..'hre not..." Oliver breathed, wheezing out the words along with all the air in his lungs in a desperate and horrid effort to assert some kind of dominance he simply didn't possess.

The man at the door bent down, gliding a rough hand over the boy's pallid face, stringing his fingers through his hair and finally resting it on Oliver's incredibly tense shoulder, causing him to flinch almost instinctively.

"You cut all your beautiful hair." The man smiled, his eyes darting around the cabin in search of something unknown.

The familiar stranger pushed past him, casually forcing himself into their home and looking around the place with sarcastic judgment. "Marie was always a fan of the quaint."

Slowly, he spun around, sauntering through the home as if he owned it, picking up framed photos of the family to quietly sneer at before setting them down. He spun on his heel to face Oliver once more as he moved to sit down on the couch.

The poor child stood entirely frozen, aside from small, uncontrollable tremors that occasionally rippled through him. Dindet stood beside him, quiet concern on her face as she tried to comprehend what was going on.

Oliver suddenly gripped her hand, clenching it tightly in his fist and wrenching her close, forcing her to swallow the brunt of his complete and utter terror as it crashed through her barrier and screamed in her head to wake up his father.

Now.

Dindet nodded, and quietly passed behind him, reluctant to leave him alone with something that scared him far more than she ever could.

But she obliged, and out of sight, quickly stepped into the In-Between to get to Jon.

"I heard about what happened," the man said, kicking his feet up and resting them on the coffee table. "You guys didn't even invite me to the funeral."

Oliver finally dragged in a quick, staggering breath, "You're not supp– supposed to be here."

A terribly delayed reaction, that the man shirked off with a light chuckle.

"Au contraire, baby girl, I have every right to see my daughter." He held up a piece of paper and waved it gently in the air before standing up again and striding toward the boy, forcing him to take a nervous step backward. "And according to the court, I legally have custody again."

Oliver gulped dryly, averting his eyes from his biological father's gaze and praying that his dad would come sprinting down the stairs.

The man pressed his lips together tightly, and drew a hand through Oliver's hair once more, threatening to tighten his tangled fingers.

"I really don't like this."

"Matthew." Jon's voice ran cold and stern, and he briskly walked toward his son, yanking Oliver away by the arm and forcing himself between the two of them. "You are trespassing on my property and if you don't leave now, I'm going to call the authorities."

Mathew blinked and straightened himself to appear slightly taller than Jon. His eyes flickered around the room, catching sight of the alien that stood confusedly next to his child, hesitantly resting a hand on his shoulder.

"Didn't think you'd be that quick with it, Jon— or were you two messing around behind my back?" He took another nonchalant step toward the two of them, causing Oliver to defensively move in front of the clown, pushing her behind and confusing her even further.

"She's cute."

"You need to leave," Jon repeated through gritted teeth. "Now."

Mathew held up his hands in mock defeat and turned slowly on his heel toward the still ajar door.

"Alright, alright, I can sense I'm not welcome." He complied, taking long strides out the door only turning just as he got to his car. "See you in court, baby girl."

There was a silent tension in the air that electrified every individual moment that began with the man's arrival and lasted long after his departure, and not a single one of them moved until they heard and saw his vehicle careen out of the icy driveway and down the long road.

Oliver's horror was so palpable that it tainted everyone in the home, mixing with deep-seated rage from Jon and lost among the whirling confusion of Dindet.

The silence felt as though it lasted hours, and she couldn't get Oliver's visceral, terrified screaming out of her head. It wasn't until

Jon abruptly rushed to his son, asking questions she didn't understand, that the clown was jerked from her stupor and made to face whatever monstrosity was left as the aftermath to this stranger's arrival.

She was merely audience to whatever it was that shook the two of them to their core, watching dumbly as Oliver trembled and shuddered and his father frantically held the stupefied boy in his arms, telling him everything was going to be fine when all she could really pay attention to was the overwhelming taste of fear.

It was delicious and she loathed it. Yet, ruminated in it until the two of them finally parted and Oliver threw on some poorly constructed facade in effort to return to the normalcy that was so suddenly stripped away from him.

"Due to negligent response you've been summoned to appear in court...to discuss the custody arrangements proposed.." Jon trailed off, lowering the letter and glancing nervously at his son who sat more than numb on the couch. "Oliver, I'm so sorry."

He didn't respond, aside from a small nod that no one aside from Dindet noticed. The clown stood awkwardly in the corner, forced into a cold realization that whatever terrible thing was happening, she had no control or understanding of. It made her insides burn with an unknowable loathing toward the stranger that upheaved their simple Saturday afternoon.

Oliver on the other hand was stiff with shock. Sitting on the couch in incredible silence while the hole inside him devoured every last bit of joy that was leftover from a mere hour ago. On occasion, he stirred, if involuntarily, but he didn't speak. There wasn't anything to say.

This wasn't the same type of fear Dindet recognized from him, not the soft terror he held for her and her wiles.

No, this was a deep-seated horror he knew and recognized with an unjust familiarity that alluded the clown's perception. Something so strong it tainted the very fiber of his being and reflected in quiet perpetuity on her face.

She moved, far more hesitant than usual, and sat next to the empty child to try and find some understanding of this visceral thing he knew and she did not.

He looked to be in a sort of trance, staring at nothing while the inside of him whirled and shrieked with a kind of agony that gently tensed every single muscle he had.

Dindet swiveled her head back to check on his father, who rubbed his eyes and face, tugging at the hair on his chin in silent effort to come to a conclusion he didn't have.

"Oliver?" Her voice was almost a whisper, tinged with worry as she attempted to rest a hand on his, only to have him jerk away, flashing a startled look at her.

"Don't—" He half breathed, catching the concern in her eyes for a quick moment. "Just leave me alone."

The boy stood abruptly and swiftly walked upstairs, escaping to the solitude of his room and shutting the door a little louder and harder than necessary. Dindet followed, only to stop at the edge of the stairs when Jon shot her an empathetic look and shook his head, prompting her to very reluctantly turn away and move back to the couch.

"I know you don't know what's going on." Jon sighed, finally setting down the letter and moving to kneel in front of the confused alien. "I'm sorry."

The man paused, choking back tears as best he could before giving up entirely and simply leaving as well, only stopping once more to utter another quiet apology before he too escaped to the attic.

I Don't Want to Talk About it

It was late now, and Jon lingered outside his son's room with a bowl of hot curry soup, hesitant to knock on the door.

It didn't make any sense, he thought. Oliver had been going about things as normally as he ever could, pretending that this was...

Jon pulled his hand back from the handle, realization slowly trickling down his spine in a horrid shiver. *This was what he was worried about. This was what he came to the attic to talk about.*

The scientist steeled himself in his thoughts, and quietly crept the door open to confront his son.

Oliver sat on his bed, curled up so tightly that he looked like a heavy rock that had been placed neatly amongst his pillows. He didn't look up when his father entered the room, only drew further in upon himself as trite shelter from what he was prepared to endure.

"Hey...Ols," Jon spoke quietly, some soft memory tracing along the image he saw. His child looked so tiny, granted he was always rather small. But it reminded him of the day he brought Oliver back from the hospital. And the first night he and Marie stayed here.

"I brought you some soup," he said, meekly holding up the still steaming meal. "It's your favorite, coconut chicken curry."

Oliver didn't answer and kept himself firmly buried in his silence.

"Dindet and I are downstairs, we wanted you to join us for dinner." His father glanced around the room, taking notice of the crumpled-up letter on the kid's nightstand. Next to a downturned family photo.

Jon let out a gentle sigh and placed the framed picture upright again, lingering for only a moment or two on their smiling faces before he set the curry down next to it.

"Ols." He moved closer, making sure to stay within easy line of sight, just in case Oliver lifted his head to look at him. "I'm not mad."

At his words, the boy dug his fingers into his skin, pushing his head deeper into the crevice of his pulled up knees. He didn't believe him.

Jon dropped down, sitting criss crossed on the floor next to his son's bed. Now wasn't a good time to try and comfort him physically, he knew if he tried, he would just scare him.

So instead, he fiddled with the edge of his blanket, trying to come up with words to say that would actually help.

"Can you say something?" he asked, glancing up at the wall of pillows Oliver had corralled himself into. "It doesn't have to be a lot, I just want to know if you can hear me."

Oliver shifted, raising his head slightly, not enough to see or be seen, but enough to be heard.

"I can." He croaked, heaving in an unsteady breath. "..I'm in trouble...aren't I?"

"No," Jon let out a gentle sigh, leaning up against the boy's bed, "no, you're not in trouble."

"But this is my fault."

"It's not your fault, Oliver," he argued quietly, glancing up at his son. The child shuddered and shook his head in silent disagreement.

"None of this is your fault, it's mine. I should have been looking out for you, and I should have listened more closely, paid more attention," Jon explained.

"But you've been so busy, I didn't want— I don't wanna bother you."

Jon couldn't help but smile slightly, though all he felt was a gut-wrenching sorrow and guilt that pervaded the room like a thick fog. "My being busy doesn't mean you can't talk to me about things that've been bugging you."

"But I ruined everything."

"You didn't ruin anything, Oliver," his father spoke softly, calmly. It wasn't often that this happened. But every single time it was warranted. "You were afraid, and you're allowed to be afraid. That doesn't mean you ruined anything."

"Yes, I did!" Oliver unfurled himself and stared at the wall, "we were- we were so close, and I screwed everything up. Just like I always do. You should be mad!"

The boy twisted around, gripping the edge of his mattress and letting his wall of pillows fall as he met eyes with his father. They were so gentle. Kind, like he didn't do anything wrong.

"You should be mad at me!" He shook, staring down at that horrible look of compassion his dad gave him. It was sickening.

"I'm not—"

"But I deserve it!" Oliver rigidly smacked his palms against his head, "I did bad! I'm bad!"

The kid hit himself, this time harder, again and again until his wrists were jerked away from him and he was forced to stop. Jon sat across from him on the bed now, tears building in his eyes as he stared at Oliver and slowly pulled the boy's hands down to his lap.

"You are not bad, Oliver," He said, his voice was so stern and soft at the same time, and for a second or two Oliver forgot that he cared at all.

"Why do you even want me?" the boy asked, dropping his gaze down to the plaid of his blankets. "You married my mom...you could've had your own kid. Why do you keep me around?"

"Because *you're* my kid. And I want *you*," Jon answered, gently brushing his son's hair out of his eyes. "Your mother was the love of my life, but you're the reason I'm still living."

"But I'm broken."

The man stared at his child, trembling and cold and empty. How cruel it was that he could say such a thing. Believe something so devastating about himself. How cruel that he lived in a world that taught him that.

"Why would you want me if I'm not..."

Oliver's voice was hollow, and he pulled away from his father, "...what anyone ever wants."

"Oliver-"

"I'm *fucked* up!" he shouted, closing in on himself in the furthest corner of his bed. "I'm messed up, you know it, mom did too, even— even Dindet knows I'm wrong. Everything about me is wrong, and broken and empty and I de– I deserve to go back with him."

"Oliver please, don't—"

"Don't what?! Say it?" The kid shot a wild glare at him, but the tears in his eyes betrayed all that convoluted pain and guilt he felt. He was a burden. To anyone and everyone around him and they deserved to know it. "You should have never taken us in."

Oliver grew calm and cold like that white-hot anger had finally given way to his sinking depression."You would have been better off, and I would probably be dead by now, so it doesn't really matter, right?"

"Mom never would have gotten that job at the lab, Matthew wouldn't be here. It's easier if I'm just out of the picture." His voice was a murmur, and every word broke his father's heart even further.

Oliver had no idea. No inkling of a clue how much he was cherished and loved.

"That's not true," Jon muttered, reaching out to pull his child close and tight in his arms. "That's not true and you know that."

He pressed his face into his son's hair, shuddering with the effort it took to keep his composure. "I know you think that...that you aren't worth it, and I hate the people who made you think that, Oliver. I really, truly do. But you are worth more than the world to me."

"I know—" Jon choked on his words, "I know I'm not the same as Matthew, or your mother. I know I'll never be the same as them to you, but I have always loved you like you were mine. That will never change. I don't care if you think you're broken, or you think that it's hopeless."

"You are my son, and I will do everything in my power to be the father you deserve." He paused, pulling Oliver away from him so he could look him in the eye. "And you deserve the absolute best."

"What's gonna happen now?" For a brief second, Oliver's eyes flickered to the letter on his nightstand. And in his father's hesitancy to answer, he came to the conclusion as well.

"I'm gonna have to go with him...aren't I?"

***

Dindet stood outside the attic door, it would have been a lie if she didn't overhear small portions of the scientist and his son's conversation. No amount of it made anything more clear though. And as Jon quietly closed the door to Oliver's room, she made haste to seem as nonplussed by it as possible.

"We need to talk." Jon's voice was quiet but direct, and he gestured for the alien to follow him. Dindet nodded, silently keeping pace with the man as he made his way back down the stairs.

She only slowed as she passed Oliver's room and the overwhelming shadow of despair that radiated from inside.

"Dindet," Jon ordered softly, directing her to step out on the back porch. She obliged and the man promptly followed, dropping down on the wooden planks like all the energy had been drained from him in a single instant.

"I appreciate all you've done to help me with my machine." He began, gliding his fingers through his hair as his thoughts grew heavier. "But I am going to need your help with something different now."

"It's about that man, isn't it?" Dindet's eyes flitted back at the scientist, he tasted awful. Some swirling mess of sour anguish and determination and it set her on edge. There was nothing good about this.

"Matthew. He's going to try to get full custody of Oliver— no doubt for a portion of the settlement the lab gave us," Jon answered, "he's got a crew of legal heads on his side, and Marie never pressed charges...so I can't count on the authorities or C.P.S. to intervene."

"You want me to get rid of him for you?" The clown rippled, some small part of her understanding the gravity of such a request. But it made so little sense. "But you made him leave before, why can't you make him again?"

Jon rubbed his eyes and let out an uneasy groan, "I know you're not familiar with human customs, but it's not that easy. I don't want you to get too worked up on the details, but I need your help convincing the judge that he is unfit to parent."

"I don't understand?"

"If you don't help me, Oliver is going to go away." Jon let out a heavy breath. "And..he's never going to come back."

At that, the alien blinked, small bits of her already flying away at the thought of it. She turned away and began plucking her fingers, rhythmically pulling pieces of herself apart as the growing unease riddled her.

He was going to go away. And not come back.

No more colors?

"I'll do whatever you want," she murmured, though her thoughts had already turned to static and the whipping frenzy of the world collided in on itself in a haze in front of her.

"Thank you." Jon's voice echoed in her head, temporarily pulling the clown from her stupor of disarray. She stared at him, drinking in the supple flavor of his sweet gratitude. "You have no idea how thankful I am."

It was untrue. She could tell exactly how grateful he was. And how ever so slightly, that deep-seated hatred he held for her and the fear he had of her ebbed away from the tide.

That wasn't what mattered in the moment though.

The only thing that mattered right then was that if she didn't do this and if she didn't do it right, she would have to start everything over again. And she really, truly, didn't want to.

No Colors

Whatever that man had brought with him, it caused a seemingly permanent change in the home. Not Oliver, nor Jon spoke about it, or if they did it was never near the clown.

"Do you wanna go somewhere?" Dindet asked, peeking out from behind Oliver's door. The boy laid in his bed, curled up in a little ball that reeked of depression and darkness, and whole desperation. He didn't answer.

Dindet slid past the door and nervously approached, leaning in effort to get a better look. She crouched down, dropping onto all fours, and scrambled to the other side of the bed where he faced toward the window.

His eyes were clenched shut and he had his arms folded over his head like he was taking cover from something invisible, and his nose scrunched up when he noticed her presence.

"Go away." He groaned, tossing himself over to face away from her once more.

Dindet crawled around the foot of the bed to the other side, resting her chin on the mattress and waiting for him to do something.

Oliver's eyes opened, only to see if she was still there, and he promptly rolled onto his stomach, burying his face into the pillows.

"No, I don't want to go anywhere," he answered finally, though his voice was muffled by the pillows. The clown let out a quiet, sad sigh and pulled away from the bed.

"Not even to school?" He had missed at least three days now, she'd been counting, and Douglass kept asking her every time he saw her why he wasn't there.

"It doesn't matter anymore." Oliver threw up a defeated hand before letting it fall down again, so he could pull a pillow over his head to wallow even more.

Dindet lowered her head and folded her arms over the bed to use them as a chin rest.

"Oliver," she whispered, "you wanna hear a joke?"

He didn't reply.

"Okay...a photon checks into a hotel and is asked if he needs help with his luggage." Dindet scooted a little closer, "he says 'no, I'm traveling light.'"

Oliver let out a pained groan and turned his head from underneath his pillow. "you're such a nerd."

Good enough, she thought, doing a triumphant little wiggle.

"You know, you can never trust an atom, they make up everything!" She giggled, settling once again to see his reaction.

This time, he sat up, taking the pillow he had over his head and pressing it into her face with a gentle enough force that she was pushed off her perch to fall over with laughter.

Dindet sat up, still humming small chuckles until Oliver's forced smile made her still, and that little joy was gone.

"I'm sorry," she preemptively said, averting her eyes. "I just wanted to make you feel better."

She folded her legs up and rocked on the floor for a moment, watching to see what he might do. He stared at nothing, and for a second or two, a shudder ran up through him, then he fell back onto his pillow.

"He's a bad person," Oliver said after a short moment of silence. He closed his eyes."He hurts people."

Dindet stopped her rocking, and leaned a little closer, realizing the subject of which Oliver now spoke.

"When I was little, we— Mom and I lived with him and it was...bad." He dragged in a ragged breath, lowering his voice to a soft, almost noiseless whisper. "I don't want to go back."

"So don't."

Oliver opened his eyes and sat back up, staring down at her with incredulity and a furrowed brow.

"You don't get it. I'm just a kid, there are rules. I don't get to decide.." he trailed off for a moment, "only grown-ups get to, and since Mom is..."

He hesitated, then slowly returned to his ball form, rolling away from the clown and digging his nails into his skin in weak effort not to choke on the tears that bubbled up from under the surface.

"She can't fix it anymore."

Dindet nodded to herself, tasting the soft return of that despair that ate at him on a near-constant basis. She picked at the carpet, thinking to herself some kind of way she could maybe do just that. Fix it.

"Why don't you just ask?" she murmured, not really contemplating why that hadn't been an option in the first place.

Oliver made a face, almost like he were in the midst of deciding whether he should laugh or cry. Or both. *She really, seriously, certainly can't possibly be that stupid.*

"I can't." He didn't have the energy to explain to her what a horrid idea it was.

"Why not?" *Apparently, she is that stupid.*

Oliver winced and twisted back around, throwing his hand out blindly and letting it hit the top of her head.

"Because..it's a really stupid thing to do." He paused, almost digging his fingers into the soft film of her form, but pulled his hand back. "it's dangerous."

Dindet lifted her head and turned to face him, despite the fact that he already had buried his face under his pillows once more.

"What if I asked for you?"

That made the kid sit up, and for less than half a second he might have contemplated it before his face turned up with an ugly scowl and he glared at her.

"Don't do that."

The alien bit her lip, averting her eyes as she twiddled. "It can't really hurt though, right? The worst that can happen is him saying no."

That is definitely not the worst thing that could happen.

Oliver stared at her for a second or two, trying to gauge if she were genuinely contemplating the idea.

"I mean, also, I think if he knew how much he scared you, then maybe he'd stop trying so hard?"

"Dindet.." He reached out, just as the clown stood up and began pacing.

"Plus, he's supposed to be your dad, right? So shouldn't he be okay about it?"

Don't do this.

"Dindet—"

"Mr. Your Dad is *also* your dad, and he made him leave before? And all he did was tell him to."

Oliver hesitated, pulling himself to the edge of the bed in order to get her attention better. "It's not like that—"

"So probably, I think if we just tell him that you don't wanna go—"

"Dindet, it doesn't work like that." He stood up, attempting to block her way as she paced back and forth. "*He* doesn't work like that."

"I know how to find him, too, cause Mr. Your Dad went to

the internetting to find him too, he's at a place I think called Ehil Inn?"

"Listen to me—" Oliver stepped in front of her, only for the alien to phase completely through him, more engrossed in her own plan than his idly growing anxiety. "Listen, it's not a good idea—"

"What room was it? 14? Or was it 27? Longitude is...I think 14.06372?" Dindet spun around, smacking her fist on her palm as she recalled the exact location he would theoretically be. She made her way toward the door, forcing Oliver to clasp his hand in hers in one last attempt to keep her from doing something very, very stupid.

"Dindet! Don't do this!"

Suddenly the door opened, and the two of them halted, blocked by Jon who stood in the doorway.

"Oliver." His voice trembled, despite the concerted effort his step-father made to conceal his torrent of anxiety. "It's time to go."

The boy relinquished his hold from Dindet and took a hesitant step back. "But I'm not ready."

"I'm not either," Jon replied, stepping aside as he patiently waited for the kid to follow. Oliver hung his head, shuffling slowly toward the door. Dindet moved as well, only for the scientist's hand to bar her from exit, prompting her to look up at him in confusion.

"I'm sorry, but you can't come with us," he said quietly, his eyes flickering back toward the look of betrayal Oliver gave him.

"Why not?"

Jon ignored his son's question and knelt down to meet eye level with the alien. "Remember what we talked about? I need you to stay here for now."

She blinked, and slowly nodded, despite every atom in her body desperately wanting to disagree.

Jon returned a stiff dip of his head and stood, gently nudging his son out the doorway as he closed the door behind him.

Dindet stared forward, some silent frenzy wiling about inside her at the thought of being here alone. All she could think of was the abrupt shutting away of all those colors that had been swirling around her, filling her tongue with flavors. And how easily they had just gone.

***

"Dad, why can't she come with us?" Oliver plopped down into the passenger seat of his father's car. "You said she was in the system, right?"

"She is," his dad answered, pulling the shift into gear. "I've got a plan though. And her coming with us today is going to make things needlessly complicated."

He backed out of the driveway and began the drive to the county courthouse.

Oliver stared out the window, watching the trees and houses pass by with increasing speed. Though his thoughts stayed firmly planted on Dindet and his father's plans.

If they weren't, they would have taken off with terrible imagined scenarios with Matthew.

"What are you gonna do?" he asked, glancing back at Jon and his increasingly tight grip on the gear shift.

"I have to prove that Matthew is an unreliable parent. So Dindet is going to help me convince the judge that he's violently unstable," he answered, biting his lip at the sheer improbability of achieving such a goal.

"Why can't you just use my medical records?" Oliver turned toward him, "from three years ago? The hospital's supposed to have all that stuff."

Jon's grip tightened on the steering wheel and he took a hard turn into the courthouse parking lot, coming to a stop at the edge of a grassy area.

"Marie..lied. On the intake forms."

Oliver's heart dropped, and a creeping despair brought bile up in his throat at the thought.

No. That's impossible. She wouldn't do something like that. She couldn't do that.

Not knowing what— what Matthew was capable of.

He was forced from his thoughts as the passenger door opened. Jon had already gotten out and moved around to his side. He stood, patiently waiting for the boy to leave. Oliver didn't want to though. He didn't want to leave this spot and everything it was.

Because, if he did, that meant he would be leaving his entire life. And going back to one he so viscerally didn't want.

***

Dindet paced around the living room of the cabin, tearing off pieces of herself in effort to calm the unbridled concern that plagued every molecule of her. It was late, she imagined. The big circle in the sky had dipped low behind the treeline, and they still weren't back yet.

The clown rhythmically pulled at herself, unconsciously ripping her fingers off and gradually moving up her arms until half of her composition floated in the air like malformed black bubbles.

They were taking too long.

The front door creaked open, and Dindet jerked around, watching the scientist's downtrodden face as he routinely put up his coat and keys. She waited, craning her neck to see where Oliver stood behind him. But there was no movement, no colors that radiated in the midst of Jon's. He wasn't there.

"Where's Oliver?" she asked though Jon seemed to ignore her completely. He kicked off his shoes and shuffled to the couch, sinking deep into it with a heavy, shaking breath.

"He's... going to stay with Matthew for a bit," he answered in a low whisper.

"But you said—"

"I know what I said." Jon plucked at his beard, glancing back at her before his gaze moved back to the nothing in front of him. "I was hoping that the judge would let him stay here, but seeing as I don't...didn't have custody...Matthew is claiming that I've been withholding visitation."

"Where is he?" Dindet paced behind him, her panic growing stronger with every step. "Where are his colors?"

"I don't understand." The scientist's voice was hollow, and he pressed his fingers into his eyes in an attempt to quell his own frustrations.

"His— his colors," she stammered, bits of her rippling and bubbling at the words. "They can't go, I'm not allowed to— where, where did you hide him?!"

"I DIDN'T HIDE HIM!!" Jon barked, causing the alien to spike at his words and draw in a ragged mock breath. He let out a pained groan and hunched forward, dragging his hands over his face in order to calm himself.

"I didn't hide him, he's *my son*. I have to get him back." The man's voice trembled, and his sudden loss of composure brought the clown to a halt. She stilled and stared at him as he bowed his head in hopeless defeat.

"I just...I need to get my son back."

Some People

Oliver hung about the outside of the bar Matthew had stopped at after court, still shuddering and shaking off the residual shock of the judge's verdict.

The man had carted him off to some skeezy back-alley pub in the next town over to 'celebrate' the occasion. But he knew this was no cause for celebration.

"Come on." Oliver grit his teeth, watching the street lights turn on in the twilight.

It had been hours now, and he couldn't get a hold of Jon at all.

He smacked his palms against the brick wall lightly, building up the nerve to go in and confront him.

He pulled in a heavy breath and spun on his heel, pushing through the pub door.

Matthew sat at a table in the corner, chit-chatting with other forty-something-year-old men between swigs of beer.

Oliver forced his way through the small crowd of tables and stools and people, coming up on his father as he laughed at some racist joke another patron made.

"It's getting late," he stated, narrowing his eyes at the man. "I have school tomorrow."

"Boys, boys." Matthew pretended to ignore him. "This is my daughter, Liv."

He wrapped his arm around Oliver's thigh, forcing the boy off balance enough that he had to lean on Matthew's shoulder to stay up. "She's a cutie, huh?"

"Baby girl, this is Eddie." Matthew gestured at the man sitting across from him, "he owns a little club down in Vegas, you know the kind."

"I don't care." Oliver's jaw clenched and he clawed into his father's hand, preventing it from straying any further than it already had. "Are you drunk?"

Matthew squeezed him with a light chuckle then let him go.

"I am," he answered, lighting a cigarette as he stood up. Oliver hesitated, forcing himself not to step away as his father neared, doubling in height and looming over him. "But I'm sober enough to get your sorry ass back to the motel."

Matthew dropped his hand on top of the boy's head and gently pushed him back, turning him around to face the door as he walked. "Come on, gotta get you nice and proper for the next hearing."

Every fiber of Oliver's body screamed to not be touched, he wanted to kick and claw and shove his way out of Matthew's reach, but at the same time, he could barely even move. And once they exited the bar, all pretense fell.

"I'm not staying with you," Oliver said, he trembled though, and the words didn't sound nearly as effective as he wanted them to. "Take me back to Jon's."

"I flew out three states to be here, I have every right to see you. Judge even agreed," Matthew retorted, opening the passenger door to his truck. "You should be grateful I even want to."

"I was grateful when you were in Vegas. Away from me." Oliver began to turn, searching the immediate area for some kind of escape route. If he had to, he would walk the some odd sixty miles to get home.

Matthew's hand wrapped around Oliver's arm before he could move though and tightened. Just enough that if he wanted to, he could break it. "What was that?"

"Nothing." Oliver breathed.

"Thought so, get in the car." Matthew loosened his grip and the kid immediately followed his instruction, sliding into the passenger seat just before his father slammed the door shut and joined him.

He revved up the engine and quickly peeled out of the parking lot, taking some winding back road to whatever place Oliver desperately did not want to go to.

Oliver fished his pocket for his phone and curled up into the door in effort to hide it from his father as he attempted to send a text to his step-dad. Matthew promptly threw his hand over him though and stole it out of his grasp.

"Olivia, I swear to god, I'm not gonna try and kill you." He barked, tossing the phone into the backseat.

Didn't stop you last time.

Matt grumbled at the lack of verbal response and rifled through the dash, grabbing something small and round and half-mindedly slapping it down in Oliver's lap, causing him to jump.

It was a little plastic chip, sort of grimy looking, but it had a big 500 on it.

"Does that make you feel better?" Matthew asked, though it didn't really sound like a question. "I stopped drinking after she took you."

You were just drinking in the bar.

Oliver hesitated, turning over the chip to see if it was authentic before the man continued, "I figured you'd think I didn't care, like I'm not sorry for what I did. But I did my time. So I'm sorry."

"I don't—"

"You're mother though, this is all her fault," Matthew interrupted, "You should be happy with yourself, but she fed into your delusions, I said– I said, 'don't Marie,' I said you were clearly not all there, you know? Things got out of hand, it happens."

Matthew pulled a right, leading them further back toward the edge of town.

"I'll make you right. No more of this pretending, pumping you full of chemicals or whatever, you're my baby girl. Ain't no one gonna take you away from me."

"I don't want that—"

"You don't know what you want, Olivia!" Matthew retorted, swerving as he veered into a motel parking lot. "You think you're happy like this—"

"I *am*."

"DON'T INTERRUPT ME!" Matthew slammed his hands into the steering wheel, and Oliver froze, closing in on himself in order to hide how hard it became to simply breathe.

"Oh, *come on,* Olivia, it was *ONE TIME.* Your mother and I argued constantly, but that's over now. She's dead. *Get over it.*"

Oliver dropped his gaze and filed his hands between his thighs in small submission. A silence fell between the two of them, filled only by the inconsistent little gasps he made in effort to quell the adrenaline in his veins.

"What you said at the bar was rude." Matthew changed the subject, putting his truck in park. "It hurt my feelings."

Oliver mouthed a small 'good' under his breath and began unbuckling his seatbelt. He wanted to be as far away from his biological father as quickly as possible, but he stopped the moment he heard the car locks click.

"You should apologize." Matthew's voice was low, and it caused a chill to run down the kid's spine.

"I'm sorry." Oliver flicked the window lock back up, only for it to pop back down with another click.

"I don't like that tone. Say it like you mean it."

"I'm sorry," Oliver repeated louder and with slightly forced inflection as he attempted to open the door once again.

Matthew threw a vicious look at him and reached out, tangling his fingers up in the boy's hair and yanking him back.

"Living with that bastard must have made you forget how to show respect!" He snarled, jerking Oliver's head back and forth until the kid's nails dug into the tops of his hands. "Is that how you're gonna talk to your father?!"

Oliver winced and drew in a small gasp at the sting. "I'm sorry! Please—"

"Are you? Doesn't sound like it," Matthew retorted. He shoved Oliver's face into the cushions and dropped the middle seat down over him, leaning on it with all the weight of his upper body and pressing the boy's head down. "Sounds more like you feel bad you got caught."

Oliver frantically flailed about in attempt to escape, panic setting in as his lungs desperately searched for air.

"Do you mean it?"

The kid smacked his hands against his father's arms and shoulders, blindly and wildly trying to grab something that he could use to get out from underneath him. He let out a muffled shriek and Matthew finally lifted the weight from his head.

Immediately Oliver sat up, heaving and retching from the rank smell of ash and smoke trapped in the fabric of the cushion. He blinked, and his eyes flickered up to Matthew before he pulled in on himself in submission.

"I– I'm sorry," he murmured, "for what I said at the bar...it wasn't respectful."

"Show me." The words dripped from Matthew's lips like poison and he wore the smallest of smirks that made Oliver's breath hitch when he recognized it.

"..Dad." his eyes flickered up to meet his father's gaze and the shaken look on his face turned into one of horror, just before he dropped his gaze.

"...Please…"

***

"No, I understand, but there should be records of the court case, it only took place three years ago. I have been diligent with providing them, as well as our marriage license." Jon paced around the kitchen island, on his tenth or twelfth call with the lawyer he had paid, and his fifth or sixth cup of coffee.

Dindet stayed in the corner though, watching him move about in fervor from her spot by the fireplace.

It was late, and he had been in and out of phone calls, or his bedroom, running around and gathering paper after paper of receipts, forms, and documents that he slapped down on the island in a messy array.

"No, listen, *you* don't understand. This man has violated our restraining order, you have records of his arrests, so why are you letting him take my son?!" Jon pressed his thumb to the bridge of his nose, holding back another frustrated grunt.

"I don't care that he had court papers! I wasn't informed about this, I am his step-father! How can you expect me to be comfortable knowing my child is staying with him when I have medical records of his injuries?! No, he's not a felon." He spun on his heel, sticking the phone between his ear and shoulder in effort to pull out documents he had picked up at the local hospital. "Oliver was discharged into my custody from Pine Valley Medical Center on June 28th, do you— no, he goes by Oliver, not Olivia. Do you know...no. No. He had to have glass surgically removed from his— Yes, and concussion. And a broken—"

Jon cut himself off with a nod, his gaze flitted to Dindet and he snapped hastily, pointing at the pen on the coffee table next to her. The clown hurried over and handed it to him, quickly getting out of the man's way as he searched for a clean flat area to scribble his notes down. "Yes, I have reason to believe she lied to protect— uh-huh. I can definitely do that. I have other– other records, transcripts, and recordings from when he was in therapy. Her name is Debra, yes, I will compile everything in a secure email. Thank you."

The scientist promptly ended the call and chucked his phone at the wall in frustration, causing Dindet to duck out of the way.

"God this is infuriating!" Jon let out a guttural noise and plopped down on the couch, prompting Dindet to edge slightly closer.

"How come they won't let him come back?" she asked, rounding the sofa slowly as some precaution against the man's nervous and frustrated fidgeting.

Jon bit at his nails for a moment, grunting quietly to himself before he worked up a more appropriate response.

"By their standards, I'm the one in the wrong...and there's not enough evidence to support my argument, yet," he answered, briefly glancing back at Dindet.

"Evidence?" The clown stood in front of him, shifting from one color to the next as she idly picked at her fingers to alleviate her nerves.

"Some people..." Jon let out a sigh and pulled his hands away from his face, wringing his fingers in small attempt to elaborate. "Hurt their children."

The alien grew still and dropped her hands to her sides. "Why?"

Jon shook his head.

"Sometimes as discipline, sometimes because they don't know better. There isn't a good enough reason why though." He leaned back, pressing the nape of his neck into the cold leather of the couch as if it would cool down his quiet rage.

"Matthew hurt Oliver." Dindet echoed the thought, bits of her spiking up in little pricks around her edges at the words.

"He hurt him very badly," Jon closed his eyes, letting out a shaky breath as the memory gained further focus in his head. "When he was smaller, and for a very long time."

The scientist opened his eyes again, turning to face Dindet with a solemn look on his face.

"That's why it's my job to get him back. Make sure he's safe."

The Undoing

Oliver stared at the motel door. Except he didn't. He wasn't actually looking at anything in the moment, or the hours that had passed in the time since Matthew had gotten out of the truck.

It was dark out though, and the soft buzzing of the streetlight rhythmically accompanied the quiet murmurs of the television through the wall.

He wanted to move. He needed to, eventually. Because if he didn't go inside soon, Matthew would be mad. *He would hurt me again.*

Oliver blinked, once, maybe twice, in effort to regain his sense of reality and closed his mouth. It tasted awful, and he shouldn't have fought back.

He numbly wiped the drool from his lips and brushed his fingers through his hair in attempt to straighten out the knots that had formed in the struggle.

Every part of him ached, throbbing and burning and he hated that familiarity.

He hated the comfort of it, and the way it crept over his skin with an agonizing gentleness.

Something that wove itself into him and whispered awful noise in his head.

The boy reached out, smacking his hand against the lever of the door in a stupid and stupefied attempt to get it to open. It clacked against the plastic though, and in his haste he pulled again, unaware that the child safety lock had been left on.

I can't stay here. With him. With that wretched monster. Jon would stop it, or Dindet, someone— someone would put an end to it. Not let it get out of hand, right?

It already had.

Oliver pushed again, harder as his thoughts whirred and buzzed around. Flying in fragmented pieces of words and pictures and terribly disgusting feelings in his head that only made the effort of just getting out so much harder.

His glazed eyes darted left and right, to the door and back, to the motel. *Did he hear me? Would he come out?*

Oliver drew in a half of a breath, in some trite effort to calm himself down. Moving so much hurt. Thinking hurt.

And his stomach twisted up in knots every time he bashed into the glass of the windows, reminding him so viscerally of the cramped and uncomfortable ways he'd been twisted and contorted up against it previously.

You shouldn't have fought back.

The thought laced itself in honey in his mind, making it sound so sweet and consoling, like his mother's own voice had said the words.

If he hadn't fought back, he wouldn't be hurting, he wouldn't be bruised and aching and trying so hard just to get out of the stupid car.

Oliver slammed his palms against the glass, letting out a stifled scream that just as quickly devolved into tears as he pressed his face up against the cold glass. *It was hopeless. All of this was—*

He blinked, his eyes gaining pointless focus on the tiny round button that was pressed into the car door. As if fate were not cruel enough, he deftly reached out and pulled the tiny thing up and the sound of the door unlocking broke the silence between the night and his unsteady breaths.

What an awful sound it was. Such a simple and sweet noise that beckoned freedom and also certain, unending suffering. And he deserved it.

In all the quiet and sickening calm, Oliver stared at the little lock, unnervingly still as something cracked and bent inside of him. It twisted and screeched, and lashed at his insides.

And in that quiet. In that sickening calm. Oliver let out a horrendous and shattered wail.

Losing himself in the uproarious agony of his own idiocy, like all the effort had been wasted in the shrill and fervent escape that never came.

He kicked and screamed and clawed at the walls and seat, heaving in foul empty breaths that only worsened the chokehold his aching and closing throat had on him.

It hurt, all of it. So much that he wanted so terribly to rip and tear at himself until there was nothing left.

So he did. Digging his nails deep into his skin in effort to peel away everything that he was and would ever be. Because all of it, *all of it*, was bad.

Oliver bit and lashed, tearing at his hair and pounding against the horrid screaming of his head.

It suffocated him, gentle and tender. A creeping blackness that darkened his vision and turned the hazy streetlights purple as it ascended up from him, silently morphing in the cold night. It came from him, planted somewhere closed off, deep and away in the recesses of his person, where he didn't want to see and didn't look.

But it was there, and with all the love and compassion of its slow and enthralling embrace, it breathed into his mind such a soft and wretched thought.

You wanted this.

Oliver shook and trembled against the comfort of the black, how it sounded so convincing in the night.

You deserve this.

He grit his teeth, sinking further into the idle concept, and its unceasing weight pulled him retching and coughing down into the floor of the truck as he buried his fingers into his skull to make it stop.

This is fine.

Some final statement, one that traced eloquently along the disjointed, nervous thoughts of his mind. It brought with it that loving quiet. The kind that made your heart still, and your eyes dull. A death that never stole any sort of personage.

It was fine.

That's all it has to be.

He could be fine with the sinking realization that there was no real escape. There was none to be made because it was fine.

I can make it fine.

Oliver stilled his shivering and tears. His dull gaze turned upward at the faint shadows of the lights as they swirled and blanketed him, sinking into his skin to join the comfort of the empty.

The blotches of the dark that clouded his eyes undulated, changing the shapes of things around him in some silent endeavor to rebuild memories he shoved deep into his psyche. It blotted out the light and brought a deafening calm to the burning of his insides and the tender parts of his skin Matthew had so viciously crammed his fists into over and over.

He stopped moving, stopped crying, and stopped caring. It was fine. *This is fine.*

One tiny little thing that would never go away. An idea that latched onto his brain and infected every aspect of him with its cool and collected few words.

It's what he deserved.

He was bad, fundamentally, intrinsically.

Matthew knew that, and he punished him for it. He deserved that punishment. And was foolish to believe that he could have anything else.

And that was fine.

Oliver dropped his gaze, slowly tilting his head toward the now unlocked passenger door. He numbly pulled the latch and the door popped open, leaking in the frigid autumn air.

The boy poured out of the truck, dropping on his hands and knees before he gathered the energy to pull himself upright and stagger to the motel door.

Quietly, he turned the knob and walked in.

"Finally." Matthew took a swig of his beer. "Almost thought you got it in your stupid head to run off."

"Least you learned one thing." He added, changing the channel from the erroneous moans and grunts to something slightly less pornographic.

Oliver closed the door behind him, keeping his empty gaze planted on the floor and only briefly flicking his eyes up to get an understanding of his surroundings.

It was a dirty, musky, double bed room, with a bathroom in the far corner and an outdated tube TV on the stand.

The whole place was a messy hovel, trash and old food littered on the ground among clothes, and various stains that genuinely he didn't want to know the origin of. Matthew sat on his bed, flipping through late-night satellite television in search of something to watch.

Oliver hung by the door, wavering in between the empty and visceral lucidity as his broken thoughts tried to piece together action or words.

"I bought you some clothes on my way here, you should try

them on." Matthew gestured at a small bag on the second bed, prompting the boy to stray from the safety of the wall toward it.

Oliver glided around the bed and pulled the plastic bag open in silence to inspect its contents.

A grossly out of season sundress, frilly and stark white, no doubt bought from an airport kiosk.

Oliver pulled the garment out of the bag, gingerly laying it out on the bed as he began to undress.

"Wait." Matthew's massive hand wrapped around Oliver's wrist, stopping him from pulling his shirt up. "Take a shower first. You smell like a wet whore and I paid good money for that outfit, I don't want you to ruin it."

Oliver let go of his shirt, patiently waiting for his father to loosen the grip on his arm. It was fine. He was used to it.

Words start to mean nothing when you hear them enough anyway.

"Are you deaf?" Matthew shook his wrist, forcing a cold answer out of the child.

"No, sir."

"Thought so, now get your ass in the shower." He let go of Oliver's wrist and smacked him hard in the back, prompting the boy to quickly move out of his immediate reach, but in such a way that wouldn't denote defiance.

"Yes, sir." Oliver turned, stiffly making his way the few more steps it took to get to the bathroom, and flipped on the light, attempting to close the door before Matthew's voice called from the other side of the room.

"Leave the door."

***

Oliver sat at the base of the tub, staring at the parts of his skin that turned purple and yellow from how often and how hard Matthew punched him in the chest and stomach. The bruises contrasted in the ugliest of ways against the rest of his skin that had turned red from the scalding shower water.

They fit nicely though, with the scars on his stomach.

They were all old, but the memory stayed fresh in his mind at all times. Permeating and coming to the front of his thoughts every time they turned to Matthew.

Oliver traced his finger along the broken circle of indentations, then covered them completely with his palm. He'd rather forget about it. *It was three years ago, so I should be over it by now. It shouldn't affect me anymore. Right?*

"You done yet?!" Matthew's voice called from the open door, followed shortly by his father barging in as Oliver frantically closed the curtain to avoid being seen.

"Almost!" He answered, pulling himself to his feet and shutting off the shower before Matthew threw the curtain open and stared him dead in the eye.

Oliver grew still and his gaze dropped to the water that had pooled around his feet. "I need a little—"

"It hurts, doesn't it?" Matthew cut in with false remorse, his eyes flickered down and back up, causing Oliver to take a small step back from him, inadvertently cornering himself in the tight space.

"It's not that bad." He lied, leaning even further away as his father moved closer. Oliver let out an unsteady breath and his eyes trained on Matthew's arms and legs as they twitched with forced restraint. "I..this isn't okay, I was—"

"What's the problem?" Matthew's hand raised, startling the kid and causing him to slip and fall back against the wall. Oliver winced and balanced himself on the handrail, taking care to move further behind the curtain to avoid him.

"I'm uncomfortable, please leave." Oliver pulled the bottom of the curtain around himself, though his focus lay solely on the ajar door behind Matthew as he rapid-fire calculated how fast he would have to move to get to it.

Matthew let out a frustrated grunt and yanked the curtain off its rail, prompting Oliver to let out a frightened little whimper as he pushed back into the corners of the shower. "Uncomfortable my ass, I changed your God damn diapers. You never had a problem before."

"I wasn't fourteen."

Matthew didn't reply, he simply pulled a cigarette out of his pack and lit it.

The bathroom filled with a heavy and disconcerting silence, enough so that Oliver dared not move from his corner of the tub, in case his father decided he wanted more from him.

"I'm sorry I hit you," Matthew finally said, taking a drag. "It's not right, hitting a woman."

Oliver held his tongue, and the man continued.

"You didn't make things easy though," he chided, in the way someone does where it doesn't sound like an insult, but definitely still cut like one. "You never do, Marie knew that."

"...Dad—"

"Let me apologize." Matthew cut him off, turning his gaze from himself in the mirror to his child in the corner, haphazardly wrapped in a moldy plastic curtain.

Oliver nodded, wringing his fingers in the curtain to keep from clawing into his own skin.

"I'm sorry I hit you."

No. You aren't.

Oliver grit his teeth in the following silence, his father wanted him to accept the apology. He always did this. No matter how bad it was, no matter how hard he hit him, or how much he made him bleed. He always apologized in the most insincere way because he never actually felt bad. He just wanted something from him.

Oliver slid down the wall, breaking the silence with the quiet sound of plastic against plastic as he curled up loosely in the bottom of the bathtub.

"I know it hurts, Olivia." Matthew put out his cigarette on the roll of toilet paper and crawled into the bathtub with him, sitting across from the boy as he kept his eyes firmly on the condensation on the wall.

Oliver didn't answer him, and he really didn't want to. He would have to eventually, though.

"Olivia." Matthew leaned in, looming over the boy as he looked away, at least until his father's fingers pressed against his chin, forcing him to meet his gaze.

"I really am so sorry I hit you," he said, pressing his fingers deeper into Oliver's cheeks. "You know I love you, and I always will. My temper gets out of control. I lost my head and I know– I know I was drinking. You probably hate me, don't you?"

Oliver stared at him with hollow, empty eyes, preparing himself for what he knew Matthew would do next. An apology from his father always came with strings attached.

"Do you hate me, Olivia?"

Yes.

"...No."

Matthew drew even closer, and Oliver instinctively pressed himself into the floor of the tub. "You want me to make you—"

"I don't." Oliver cut in, pulling Matthew's hand away from his face. "I don't want to do that...please."

His father sat back on his knees, and his face shifted from that false compassion to a quiet rage. "You think you're big and tough now, don't you?"

Oliver dropped his gaze and attempted to close further in on himself, only for Matthew to wrap his hands around the boy's wrists and prevent him from forming any protective position.

"I-I'm sorry, I didn't mean it!" He immediately backtracked, desperately trying to pull out of his father's grasp.

"No, I think you did," Matthew glared at him, tightening his grip against Oliver's trite struggling. "You think you're a big boy now."

His father yanked his arms up, forcing Oliver to awkwardly position himself at an angle in effort to stay as far from him as possible, only to be slammed back against the connecting lip of the tub and surrounding wall.

Oliver heaved in a staggered breath in an attempt to draw in the air that was forced out of his lungs. He winced and hissed, cracking open his eyes to his father's face.

He sat over him, twisting the skin of his wrists as he pressed his hands against the lip of the tub. He bent down, his lips twitching as he formed ugly words in his mouth.

"Since you're a man now..." his breath filled Oliver's senses with the stench of fresh ash. Though it wasn't even close enough to drown out the overwhelming panic that burgeoned in his chest and made his heart race as Matthew finished his sentence in a low whisper.

"Since you're a man now, I don't have to hold back."

Be Good

D ouglass stood a few feet from Oliver's front porch, the kid already missed the presentation of their group project. And hadn't come to school for almost the entire week following.

"Dindet!" he called, catching the clown's attention as she quietly rounded the porch. She looked different though now, maybe her clothes had changed. He wasn't quite sure. But the girl looked dull and tired. Her face paint that usually resembled the petals of a flower instead streaked jaggedly across her face, making her look perpetually afraid.

"Is Oliver coming to school today?" he asked and for a second or two Dindet tensed, but gave a small smile.

"I don't know." She stepped down from the porch into the couple of inches of snow on the ground and began the walk to the bus stop.

"Do you know when he plans on coming back?" Douglass kept pace with her, despite the alien's effort not to give away any information. "Or if he's feeling better?"

"I don't know."

"Is he in the hospital again?"

What?

Dindet halted, and turned to the boy, her false smile dropping for a moment as she milled through thoughts on why that word was already Familiar to her.

"What do you mean?"

Douglass shrugged, and began to shift from his general flavor of friendliness to something darker, but also soft, hidden behind a wave of compassion the alien could taste in the air around him.

"Well, I mean, when he first moved here he was in the hospital for a while, it's how I first met him— on accident," he explained, "I was actually there to say hi to my sister— I called him a vampire cause he was hooked up to a bunch of those blood bags?"

He laughed lightly at the thought. "He got so butthurt over it. But that was like, three years ago, so he probably doesn't even remember."

"He's not at one of those," Dindet answered solemnly, continuing on her slow walk toward the edge of the road.

"Have you met Oliver's other dad?"

Dindet halted, and for a second, she wiled out of control at the question. *Does he know?*

Douglass was walking beside her, kicking the gravel stones through the snow and not really noticing how deeply uncomfortable she became.

"I only ask cause that's the only reason he'd be so weird," he continued, stopping to look back at her just as she regained control. "I don't know if you knew, but Jon isn't like his biological dad or whatever. He just married his mom."

"Biological?" Dindet repeated, running through as many ideas as she possibly could to try and change the subject.

"Yeah, I've never met him, but the first time I met Ols, he was super jumpy and freaked out all the time. I just kind of figured that something bad happened and that's why they came here?"

This time, Dindet moved closer, catching up with Douglass as he made his way to the bus stop. "Something bad? Like..something that scared him a lot?"

"Well." Douglass paused. "I don't know for sure, cause he never really said, but usually when you bring it up, he gets really freaked out, kind of spacey and shaky, you know? And sometimes...I dunno, it's sort of hard to explain, and I don't think he'd be particularly jazzed about me telling you."

"Is there a way to fix it?"

"It's not...uh, well—" The kid stopped at the edge of his driveway, stalling out as he tried to better explain. "I mean, probably? He doesn't ever let anyone see him like that, so it's sort of hard, and the only reason I did was cause..."

Douglass slowed, losing his polite demeanor as his genuine concern revealed itself. "I'm just worried about him...is all."

The clown let out a soft sigh, at a loss as to what to do, if she could do anything at all, that is. *She didn't understand this person. What he wanted, no. She knew what he wanted.*

He wanted to take Oliver away.

But she didn't want that.

***

Oliver stared at the student files on Mrs. Bradshaw's desk, they were that thick manilla paper that he couldn't find in any type of art supply store. The kind that made pencil sketches look nice. Focusing on them kept his mind off the way Matthew held his shoulders, digging his thumbs in between the ruts of his spine in a discrete way, to make sure he didn't do or say anything out of turn.

"As you can see, the judge and county clerk released an official statement, and I'm very concerned about my daughter's wellbeing." Matthew smiled and said things so nicely, in such a way that he actually looked like a very caring father. He was not.

"I'd like to have the files on her amended, so there's no confusion when we transfer schools," He finished. The counselor looked up past her readers at him, her eyes briefly flickering toward Oliver as she pulled the files back to inspect.

"Is this what you want too, Oliver?" she asked.

"Olivia," Matthew corrected, digging his thumbs further into his son's spine and prompting him to answer.

"Yes, if you can.." The boy hesitated, balling up his fists in the skirt of the stark white dress Matthew forced him to wear. "Please change them all back."

"Is there a reason for this decision?" Mrs. Bradshaw nodded, pulling out a small sticky note, and began scribbling down information on it.

"I was wrong is all," Oliver lied, "but I know better now."

The counselor let out a sigh, sounding more frustrated than anything else. "Alright, I've made a note for your file, and I'll email the teachers before the bell rings."

"Thank you so much." Matthew offered a smile that was only returned with an incredulous look from the woman. "Well, we'll get out of your hair now."

The man nodded to himself and loosened his grip on his child, allowing him to freely make his way out of the door.

"See?" Matthew's voice dripped with insincerity. "That wasn't so hard now, was it?"

Oliver kept his head low, every part of him wanted to dissolve into a puddle like Dindet, but that simply couldn't happen.

"Was it?" His father prompted, leading him down the hall toward the front entrance.

Oliver breathed a humbled 'no' and trailed behind him with his fists clenched tightly to his sides. To the point that he could feel the sting of his nails digging into his palms.

"Schools about to start..." Oliver mumbled, his eyes flickering up at the few students that had begun trickling in from early morning sports and band practices. "I should get to class."

In truth, he just wanted to get the day over with. Court was this afternoon, and he wanted so terribly to see Jon and Dindet. Even if it meant he'd never see them again.

"You'll start class when I say you can."

"But—"

Matthew swiveled around, grabbing Oliver by the wrist as he jerked him off balance and thrust him into the corner of the emergency lock doors. "Listen here you little *bitch*, I paid a lot of money to fly out here just to get your sorry ass. So you're going to do what I ask when I ask you to and be a *good girl*."

Matthew shook him and Oliver brought his hands up in weak attempt to push back, pressing his palms into his father's chest as he lurched closer. His eyes flickered up, noticing the hallway camera at the furthest most corner of the wall and he drew in a quick gasp, only for Matthew to wrap his hand around his face and force him to look back at him.

"Do I make myself clear?" His voice dropped and the hand that gripped Oliver's shoulder moved lower, pulling down the loose collar of his dress to reveal the massive bruise underneath. "Or did last night's lesson not sink in?"

The boy's breath caught in his lungs and he clawed at Matthew's wrist in an attempt to lift the pressure of his fingers digging into the already tender skin.

"We-we're on camera!" Oliver wheezed out the words, but the man only let up the moment he heard footsteps echoing down the hall.

Matthew pulled back, dropping his hands down and instead wrapping them around his son's wrists. "You know I love you, Olivia."

He spoke in such a way that lingered on truth. Oliver knew that. And he knew that it meant something entirely different and wrong.

The child pressed himself into the corner, leaning as far away as he could with his father looming over him.

"I care so much about you, more than that lab rat ever will." Matthew swung his child's hands rhythmically, moving his fingers up and down the contour of his elbows until Oliver tried to pull away; at which point his grip tightened once more. "I just want what's best for you. You don't make it easy."

Oliver turned his head, staring at the pile of crickets that crawled around in the corner of the wall. *He was right. I make it so hard for anyone to care. I deserve to be punished for that. I deserve to be hurt.*

"I'm sorry I hurt you, Olivia." Matthew pressed his cheek into the boy's neck, and the breath of his words sent a terrible shudder down Oliver's spine. "I missed you so much."

Oliver quietly filed his hand between himself and the man, forcing him to hover inches away.

"Please don't...I'm at school."

***

Douglass dropped down off the last step of the bus, patiently waiting for Dindet to follow. He was at a loss. The girl wouldn't talk to him at all, let alone about Oliver.

She probably hates me. For being so concerned about Ols right after I ruined our date at the park.

He smacked himself with his palm. *You look like such an idiot! No wonder she isn't talking to you!*

"Oh my god, did you see?"

Douglass turned, overhearing some girl gossiping with her friend as they walked back from the gym.

"I did, it was crazy, I saw her with this older guy in the hall—actually wearing it!" The other girl said though she hushed up just as quickly as they passed Dindet.

"Don't they live together?" The girl whispered now, failing to hide the snide and curious stare she gave Dindet as they headed toward the cafeteria.

"Do you think, maybe..." Douglass trailed off, not quite sure if what he wanted to say would help. "Do you think they might have been talking about— uh, Dindet?"

He stopped, at some point, she had disappeared and left him wandering the halls alone with a dumb look on his face.

"You look poopy." Cassidy's matter-of-fact voice drew the kid's attention and she unceremoniously shoved a piece of paper in his face to look at. "Good, because your boyfriend almost made us get a C on the Poe project."

"W-what?!" Douglass sputtered, turning bright red as he took the poorly written paper and strategically kept it over his nose to hide the flush of his cheeks. "I– I don't— It's not anything like that!"

"Well." Cassidy waved away his embarrassment. "It doesn't matter anyways, I convinced Mrs. Hargreaves to give us separate grades. Since he no-showed on the day of presentation."

"I don't even think he likes boys."

The girl paused, ignoring him and glancing around in search of the most colorful thing usually present. That wasn't. "Where's Dindet?"

Douglass shrugged, doing his best to shirk off the prospect Cassidy had just shoved into his head.

"Dunno, she was just here a few minutes ago," he answered, heading off to the cafeteria. It wasn't strange for Oliver to run off on his own, but Dindet hung around him or Cassidy on a constant basis. So her dejected demeanor spiked every internal radar of Douglass's that said something was simply not right.

"I think something happened? Like at home I mean," he said, pulling out a few spare dollars for the breakfast line. "Oliver doesn't usually miss school this much, and every time I ask Dindet about it she gets all quiet."

"Yeah, probably has something to do with—" Cassidy halted, causing the boy to butt into her on what he thought was a walk to the cafeteria. But the girl stopped just outside of it, her attention squarely placed on the counselor's office and the clown that crept past the door.

"Dindet!" she shouted, causing the alien to jump at the sudden noise. Dindet swiveled her head around with a wild, startled look that immediately turned to some false sweet smile as Cassidy ran over to her.

"You did such a good job on the project! I know English isn't your first language, but you did a really, really good job standing in for Oliver. I'm so proud of you!" Cassidy sang her praise, though Dindet looked thoroughly disinterested in the display.

"What were you doing in the counselor's office?" Douglass stepped in, picking up on the fact that it made such little sense for her to be there. *Unless something was going on.*

The clown stared at him, then immediately folded in on herself, dropping eye contact.

"You really think I did good?" she said to Cassidy, deliberately ignoring Douglass in the process.

"Of course I did! English is one of the hardest second languages to learn!"

Douglass took a step back. *This isn't going to work. She clearly has absolutely no intention of talking to me or telling me anything.*

"I'll see you guys later," he said, heading off toward the classroom. Though the moment he started walking, the two girls quickly caught up with him, chit-chatting about everything and nothing. Or at least Cassidy was. Dindet mostly nodded along.

It's nuts. How could they not have that terrible sinking feeling that something was wrong?

Douglass pulled the classroom door open with a small sigh, and halfheartedly gestured for the two girls to enter before him.

Abruptly, Dindet drew in a jagged breath, clambering past Douglass and forcing her way through the door.

"Oliver!" She sprinted into the room, lunging over the desks in front of her to get to him as quickly as possible.

The boy's head jerked up and he let out a quick gasp, scrambling from his seat as she slammed her palms down on his desk, ready to hurdle over it. But she stopped and cocked her head in confusion.

"I thought only girls wear dresses?"

Something Rotten

Oliver's face twisted up for a second and his eyes flickered back to the entrance of the no longer empty classroom, and the grave, shocked look that Douglass and Cassidy gave him.

"Boys can wear dresses too sometimes," he answered softly, lowering his voice further as he spoke only to the clown. "Matthew made me…. put it on."

Douglass shook the startle from his face, offering a trite but rigid nod as he moved to take his seat. Cassidy though, for a moment, couldn't help but stare in confusion until he poked her out of her stupor. At which point, she too moved to her chair.

"Are you feeling better now?" Douglass asked, scratching his nails idly on the chipped part of his desk to distract himself and not cause Oliver even more discomfort.

"Yeah..sorry I messed up on the project." Oliver offered a meek nod and sat back down, glancing up at Dindet and prompting the alien to take her seat behind him.

"It's alright," Cassidy piped up, "I was just telling Douglass that I got Hargreaves to give us separate grades on account of you missing."

"That's cool." Oliver's voice was quiet and empty. "thanks Cas."

He kept his head low as other students began trickling into the classroom.

"Oh look, it's the resident—" Theo stopped mid-sentence at the utterly dejected and defeated look Oliver gave her. She sat down, for once keeping to herself.

Class went on as usual. A gauntlet of knowing things and learning things that Dindet wholeheartedly did not care a single ounce about. Her mind was entirely engrossed in her thoughts.

Jon said she wouldn't see him again. But he was right there, acting so...regular. like not a thing had changed.

But she could so easily taste the frenzy of darkness that lashed and whipped up against the rest of the feelings in the room.

Black as the abyss she was pulled into existence from, and swirling in a hurricane just under the surface.

"Oliver?" She reached toward him and the kid's wave of empty spiked up jagged with the abominable flavor of fear as he instinctively flinched, causing the clown to withdraw.

"Dindet." The boy pulled his arms close to himself, not raising his head or even turning to look at her. "Please.. don't touch me right now."

***

Douglass kept silent, the entire class did, aside from one or two students murmuring to each other in quiet whispers. It was like every single one of them could feel the waves of black emptiness emanating from Oliver as he sat silently in his seat, waiting for the lunch bell to ring. And then for school to eventually end.

The boy looked miserable, more than miserable. In that familiar way that Douglass recognized was so clearly reminiscent of the way Oliver looked and acted just after he moved next door.

I need to know what's going on.

"Okay class, after lunch, we're going to start on some short stories—" Mrs. Hargreaves was cut off by the lunch bell and before she could finish her sentence, students were already filing out of her room in effort to get to the lunch lines before they got too long.

Douglass stood up, glancing back at Dindet and Cassidy in silent motion to go ahead without him. He moved to the door, patiently waiting for his friend to come out as the other two left.

The teacher let out a small huff and sat at her desk, momentarily looking over papers to grade until she caught sight of Oliver, who still sat cemented to his chair.

"Mr. Tarsul, are you planning on spending the entire lunch period in my classroom?" she asked, leaning down to pull out a lunch she had packed for herself.

"I'm not really hungry," Oliver answered, keeping his eyes on the printed linoleum tree lines of his desk.

"Your friend is waiting for you though," she replied, giving a brief look back at Douglass who smiled uncomfortably. "Unless you both plan on joining me for lunch today?"

Oliver peeled his gaze away from his desk, glancing up at Douglass. He sucked in a reluctant breath.

"Okay."

He stood up, sheepishly rounding the isle of desks as he passed Mrs. Hargreaves and met up with Douglass at the door.

"You're really not going to talk about it, are you?" he asked, attempting to keep up with Oliver's increasing pace and disregard of his concern. "You missed like a week and now—"

"I know, Douglass!" He spat, "but I'd rather just deal with it than do anything because if I say something, it's just gonna make it worse."

"I've got enough to deal with already." He followed, far quieter.

"What's gonna be worse?" Douglass remarked rather incredulously, attempting to wall Oliver off before he got to the cafeteria.

"Oliver."

"Nothing, it's not your problem," he answered dryly as he spun out of the way to get through Douglass's poorly thought out barricade.

"Except it is," Douglass argued, "you miss class, Dindet is being all weird and now you show up in a—"

"So what?" He cut in, "I can do what I want, guys can wear dresses if they—" Oliver slammed hard, directly into someone's tray full of food, and stopped dead in his tracks.

"Oliver," Theo pulled her wasted tray away from him with a dazed expression on her face. "I...I didn't mean to—"

"Why would you do that?!" Oliver shouted, despite the fact that he still shook from the shock. "You—"

He stopped, and a flicker of horrid realization flitted across his face. "He's gonna think I did it on purpose."

There it is.

A single sentence that alluded to everything Douglass so desperately wanted to understand.

"Who is?" He stared at him, watching the kid slowly devolve into his mind.

Oliver bit his lip, murmuring something incredibly quiet to himself as he spun backward and went straight for the bathroom, leaving both Douglass and Theo in a quiet stupor.

"S-sorry," Douglass turned to the girl and apologized for him, then quickly followed after Oliver.

His mind raced, picking pieces of his memories apart and adding them all up in effort to figure out just what was going on. Oliver was a quiet kid, yeah, but parts of him were loud. Practically screaming in your face and he felt so stupid for not understanding why.

"Come on, come on!"

Douglass stopped at the entrance of the one unisex bathroom in the entire school, overhearing the kid and his desperate attempt to get the food and grime off the dress.

He moved, hesitation briefly preventing him from opening the door the boy must have forgotten to lock in his haste.

"Oliver what—" Douglass froze and Oliver drew in a staggered breath, suddenly dropping to his knees at the startle of the door opening.

Douglass's agape mouth clamped shut and he quickly let himself in, shutting and locking the door behind him. The sight he saw was stomach-turning, and regardless of how much he wanted to move closer to help his friend up, he stayed plastered against the door, his eyes scanning every inch of blackened skin.

"How did you get those bruises?"

Such a simple question. An awful question to have to ask.

Oliver silently reached up to the still running sink and tugged at the skirt of the dress, letting it fall over him and slosh the tiles with the water retained from his failed efforts.

"Just ignore them." His voice was a murmur, and he didn't turn around to look at Douglass at all.

"Did you fall? Run into a door?" There was a bite to Douglass's rhetorical question, and his clenched fists dug his nails into his palms at the excuses he was ready to hear.

"......Yeah."

Douglass shook his head, ready, so unbelievably ready to yell and scream at the kid for not saying anything, not telling him.

That wouldn't help though. So instead he pulled in a shaky and forcefully calming breath and began taking off his shirt and pants.

Oliver's head dipped for a second, and he swiveled it around, hearing the disgruntled and hasty effort the boy put into getting undressed as quickly as possible.

"Douglass..?" He trembled, causing him to slow his pace. "Wh-what are you doing?"

"Trade me," Douglass stated matter of factly. He balled up his shirt and pants and thrust them out in offer. "Yours is all wet and you look miserable."

"But—"

"What?" Douglass cut in, with a gentle, albeit forced smile. "Boys can wear dresses if they want, right?"

Oliver stared at him, then quickly dropped his gaze.

"You clearly don't want to." Douglass crouched down, inching closer to the boy as he gently pulled the dirty, wet garment off of him, replacing the covering with his oversized shirt. "But I think I wanna try it out today."

It was the absolute least he could do. He wanted to do more. To make it stop altogether.

He watched as Oliver slowly pulled his shirt and pants on, keeping his head ducked and turned from him in such a way that he couldn't see the boy's face.

Douglass pulled the wet dress over his head, forcing the tight fit of it down his torso despite the water traction making it harder. Oliver was smaller than him, by about half a head, and shaped a lot differently, but the pretty cotton fabric did a decent job stretching to meet expectations.

He let out a shaky breath and forced a small laugh.

"Honestly?" Douglass turned in the mirror. "Not half bad, I feel so fancy."

Oliver stood upright, staring into the mirror alongside the boy as he twisted and twirled to make the stained dress billow.

"Thank you...Douglass," he whispered, pulling his arms up in a trembling and brief moment of composure.

"It's no big—" Douglass staggered back, caught entirely off guard by the tight and heavy hug Oliver gave him. The boy shook and trembled, tightening his grip as he buried his face into Douglass's chest, mixing his tears with the wet of it.

"Hey...it's no big deal."

"No," Oliver retorted softly, pressing himself further into his friend. "it is, so— so thank you."

Douglass drew in a small breath, his heart beginning to race at how long he had been held for. This was the first time Oliver had ever done such a thing, and he was entirely unprepared. He gently moved his hands to the boy's shoulders to pull him away.

"I'm just trying to be a good friend, is all," he said, feeling his stomach twist up in knots at the words. "You deserve that."

Oliver nodded rigidly, though his fingers still tangled into Douglass's skirt, keeping him there while he regained some semblance of composure. He made a face, subtle but it was filled with enough liquid self-loathing that Douglass knew he didn't believe the statement at all.

Douglass hesitated, idly fidgeting until he gathered up the nerve to step out of Oliver's reach and toward the door.

"Well, uh, I– I've got some leftover cash from helping at the antique shop, if you wanna get like, like an ice cream from the snack stand?" He backed up, blindly throwing his hand out in a couple failed attempts to open the bathroom door.

Oliver let go of him and took an awkward step back, gesturing at the door with a slightly less sad half-laugh. "It's still locked."

His friend quickly grew flush. "Right, I knew that."

Douglass spun around so he could actually see what he was doing and pulled the door open with a nervous chuckle.

"I heard the fudge bars were pretty good, but I've never had any extra change for one before."

"Hey, Douglass?" Oliver tugged at the boy's skirt, preventing him from escaping with all the butterflies in his stomach just yet. Oliver's eyes had once again placed themselves around his feet.

"Can you please..not tell Dindet?" he murmured, dropping his grip on him. "It'll make her upset, if she knows, and I don't want her doing anything...reckless."

Douglass turned to face him and offered a small smile of reassurance. "I won't tell her if you don't want me to."

He absolutely planned on telling the counselor though.

"Thank you."

My Monsters and My Friends

It was a kind thing Douglass did. Oliver wanted to scream at him for it though. And he didn't know why.

Part of him thought it might have been because he knew that when Matthew saw him in different clothes, he was going to be hurt. He wasn't sure if the brief levity of temporary comfort would be worth what his biological father would do to 'correct' him.

Douglass didn't know that though, and Oliver preferred to keep it that way. He was far more occupied by the entity that could read every thought in his head with little more than a brush of fingers against him.

Oliver kept his gaze on Dindet as he stood in the lunch line with Douglass. She stared back at him from the table, noiseless and patient- probably trying to figure out what really was going on.

It was one thing for her to see the emptiness that permeated him like a thick fog, he knew that wasn't something he could hide. But he was horrified by the prospect of her seeing in gross and visceral detail why it was there.

Oliver blinked, focusing on the chocolate popsicle that had casually been presented in front of him by Douglass.

"It's chocolate, is that alright?"

"Uh..yeah.." Oliver took the sweet from him and numbly walked off.

***

"Is everything alright?" Cassidy's voice popped up from behind Douglass, interrupting the distracted gaze he held as his friend meandered away toward the courtyard.

"What do you mean?" Douglass grabbed a tray from the line, contemplating if he really ought to loop the girl in on what he figured Oliver wanted to keep under wraps.

"You know what I mean, Douglass. I'm not an idiot," she retorted, grabbing two trays instead of one as she followed him through the food bar. "You traded clothes."

"Matthew came back," Douglass answered, hoping that only that would suffice. He didn't really know much about him. Just that he was Oliver's biological dad, and he wasn't a good one.

At most, he assumed Matthew was the reason he and Marie moved next door in the first place.

Oliver rarely deliberately mentioned the man. But when they first moved there, and Oliver was in the hospital, there would be a beat-up rusty truck on the side of the driveway every afternoon when Douglass walked home. He never saw anyone in it.

"Matthew?"

"He's Oliver's other dad." Douglass paid for his food and left the cafeteria line. Cassidy followed quickly behind him, balancing two trays in her hands as they weaved through the tables to the one they designated as their own.

"Cas." Hailey's voice gave the two kids pause as they set their food down, and the girl sauntered over with a perturbed look on her face. "You're not gonna sit with us, *again*?"

"Yeah, if that's cool? I wanted to get a tray for Oliver cause he left the line too early," she answered. Her friend's face scrunched up in disagreement, but she simply nodded and whipped around to leave.

Douglass searched the cafeteria for the subject in question, but both he and Dindet were nowhere to be seen. *They must have run outside while me and Cassidy got food.*

"I don't think he's really in the mood for lunch right now," he mentioned.

"Yeah, but you guys spent a bit in the bathroom and there won't be anything left if he goes through later." Cassidy shrugged and picked up the extra tray. "I just wanted to do something nice for him, that's all."

***

Oliver made haste to escape the noise of the cafeteria, wandering around the hedged courtyard as a very light sprinkling of rain began to fall around him. It was loud in there, and he didn't want to be seen.

People were going to talk about him.

He plopped down on the ground in the corner between a large empty dumpster and the hedge wall surrounding the courtyard and idly plucked at the dying grass around him.

He was going to miss it. And miss Jon, and Douglass and the huge conifers that dappled the mountains around him.

Matthew told him they were leaving. Moving down to Las Vegas for a 'business opportunity'.

Leaving didn't really scare him. Neither did getting hurt. The scariest part of all of this was how...comfortable he was with it.

Like the last three years had only been a fever dream and he was going to wake up with blood and glass in his stomach, and Matthew would be sitting on the apartment balcony smoking a cigarette.

"Oliver?"

"Go away Dindet." He stopped picking at the grass and his eyes focused on the shadow the clown cast over him. She stood a foot or two away, quietly rippling in effort not to eat his empty.

"You changed your skin again."

He didn't have the energy to correct her, but the comment made him raise his head to look at her.

"I really want to be alone right now," he said, turning his head away to the wall.

"Are you gonna come back?" Dindet asked, dropping down in front of him to let him know she wasn't going anywhere any time soon. "Mr. Your Dad said you wouldn't come back, but you're here."

Oliver let out a soft sigh and pulled his knees up to his chest.

"It's bad right?" The way she said it sounded far more like a statement than a question, and Dindet gestured at something he couldn't see. "The empty."

Oliver stared at her. She looked so calm and quiet, but the paint around her face had shifted, blurring and streaking into spikes and tears, and squiggles that made it hard for him to tell if she were eating his feelings or her own.

"No, I'm not coming back," he answered finally, dropping his gaze again.

Dindet inched forward, lifting her hand in effort to reach for him but the boy leaned away.

"Don't touch me." He breathed, pressing himself up against the bricks.

The clown stopped and blinked at him in confusion. "Why not?"

I don't want you to see it. I don't want you to know. Oliver grit his teeth, opting not to say the words.

"After court, I'm moving away," he said instead, "that's why I'm not coming back. To the cabin, or to school, or to Pineton."

"But you're here right now?" she argued softly, "you can just come back with me, no one will know? I can move you in the In-Between."

"He will know." Oliver closed his eyes, trying not to imagine how livid Matthew would be when he found out he ran off.

"I can hide you if you want? There are a lot of places— not just in this dimension too!" The alien offered a hopeful smile that did nothing to deter Oliver's defeated conviction.

"He will just—"

"I know! There's a place that's really fun and no one goes to," Dindet cut in, grabbing Oliver by the hand and pulling him up before he could contest, "everything is made...of..."

The alien trailed off and came to a halt, prompting Oliver to try and tear out of her grasp, but her fingers locked around his wrist and tightened as she stood in deafening silence.

"Dindet." Oliver pulled back. "Let go."

The clown's grip only tightened, as if she were becoming a solid that kept him trapped there, praying that she wasn't in his mind yet. But her head turned, rigid and slow, and she stared at him with a look that only meant one thing.

"Please." He drew in a quiet gasp and yanked against her hold. "it's not that bad, I swear."

"I swear—"

The words caught in Oliver's throat and his eyes flickered down to her claws that had melded into his skin, seeping black viscous tendrils into his veins.

The moment he looked back up, the alien's eyes turned an awful black, and a soft static built louder in his head as she read his thoughts.

"LET GO!" Oliver jerked back, stumbling from the abrupt lack of her holding him there, and whipped around at the sudden silence that fell between him and the static of Dindet's mind.

She had vanished.

"Din– Dindet?" Oliver scanned the area, trying to figure out if she left— if she went to find Matthew. Then his attention fell on something small and orange.

It sat on the ground in front of him looking like a painted rock. But as he crouched down and picked the tiny hot thing up, it was soft and pulsing. Like a heart.

He stared at it for a moment or two, trying to wrap his mind around what just happened and get rid of the ringing of his ears.

Then it dawned on him.

"Get out." The boy's voice was little more than a whisper, and his eyes flickered from the orange thing in his palm to the streaks of black that rapidly swelled under his skin.

"Dindet, get—"

A horrendous static erupted in his head, shrieking and screaming and exploding as the alien invaded every crack and crevice of his psyche. It was devouring him, feeding on his thoughts as the mass and matter it was made of spiked and jutted out of his skin.

Oliver reared back, clapping his hands over his ears in some misguided attempt to quell something that only existed in his mind. Inside of him.

It bubbled and broke, splattering on the ground like fresh blood and quickly congealing as it grew and reformed, stringing and attaching itself to him.

"GET OUT!!" He cried, tearing and pounding at his skull in effort to get her to stop cleaving through his thoughts and memories with violent rampage.

"GET OUT OF MY HEAD!!"

Oliver let out an agonized shriek and the beast screeched alongside him, turning his vision black as it burst out spitting and clawing at the ground, entirely consumed by his rage and hatred and fear and despair.

He was latched to it, screaming and clawing in the mess of it and its wild frenzy of carnage and veracity.

He was trapped by Dindet's visceral consumption of his deepest and darkest thoughts and feelings... and memories.

***

The tray in Cassidy's hands clattered on the ground and she stared in absolute horror and bafflement at the monstrous thing in front of her. Oliver was somewhere inside of it, and she could hear his guttural shrieks under the metallic and shrill cries of the enormous, black and fiery creature that had entirely enveloped him.

The monster's talons slammed into the grass, tearing it up as it prepared and launched itself into the air, vanishing the moment it became airborne.

The girl slid down, landing hard on her knees in the dirt and kept her glazed eyes on the place it was, and just as quickly stopped being.

Her eyes flickered down to the tray and food that had spilled on the ground, and she numbly reached for it, only stopping to see how she shook and trembled from the unnatural entity that had just taken Oliver.

It doesn't make any sense. It couldn't have been real, right? No. It was. She could hear him screaming the entire time. She wasn't blind and the marks in the ground were proof enough to guarantee that whatever that thing was...was real.

Her mind raced, but she moved slowly, taking the wasted food and placing it back on the tray as she sifted through some kind of conclusion to what happened.

The only other person there was me right? He ran off just after coming back from the restroom. Where is Dindet?

Cassidy stared at the apple in her hand, digging her fingers into the skin of it as she recollected everything she possibly could about the strange girl that had started living with him. How secretive she was about where she came from, even to a fellow immigrant. And the way Oliver kept watch over her like a hawk. Like they were hiding something.

Cassidy's grip loosened on the apple and she set it down on the tray, finished putting it back together, and finished with the discombobulated and incongruous thoughts in her head.

Whatever that thing was, she was absolutely certain.

It was Dindet.

I am Far more Hungry than You

Oliver hurtled through the air or another dimension. He wasn't entirely sure, and he didn't really have time or the capacity to care. He couldn't see anything except the whipping black of the alien around him as she launched them further through wherever it was they were going.

He was nothing more than the unwilling battery that fueled the clown's unbridled rage, and she was the conduit of every awful thing he kept pushed deep down and away from everyone. Especially himself.

He wasn't entirely sure if she still existed at all. All he could hear was shrieking and static dotted with his own anguished thoughts, that just as quickly cut out the moment she devoured them and replaced them with horrid memories in his head.

For a moment, the lashing darkness flickered away and he saw Matthew's shocked face as the creature crashed back into his dimension and crushed the man with its undulating and screaming mass.

"YOU MONSTER!!" Dindet's voice echoed, bellowing and shaking the glass of the windows. She forced the grown man into the In-Between, bathing everything in a soft purple hue that juxtaposed against the vicious nightmare that dug its claws into the carpet around Matthew's neck.

Oliver's blackened eyes shot open as his head filled with the startled and terrified thoughts of his father and he blindly reached out for something, anything to make the beast stop whatever it was doing.

"What the—"

"DO YOU ENJOY IT?!" The creature's voice cut through Matthew's and it let out an awful roar, spitting black viscera in his face and causing the helpless man to let out a mortified cry as he scrambled under its weight and struggled to free himself.

"LOOK AT WHAT YOU HAVE DONE!" The alien reared back, stabbing into its host's mind and forcing up Oliver's memories, shoving them to the front of his mind for Matthew to see and feel in visceral detail.

Oliver let out a horrendous cry and pressed his shaking hands into his eyes to try and block out the horrible things he was seeing, but it only grew louder with the static and screaming in his head.

Matthew shrieked and bucked, throwing his hands through the massive semi corporeal beast in a wild attempt to get it off of him. But it only made itself heavier, narrowing its blinding white eyes in disgust.

"SHUT UP AND TAKE IT LIKE A MAN!!" the animal screeched the repeated words in its host's memories back to Matthew and Oliver let out an agonized howl.

He clawed at the floating and gushing matter of Dindet.

"STOP! IT HURTS!"

"THAT IS WHAT YOU SAID!!" The alien ignored his pleading and opened its razor-sharp maw, closing in on Matthew's head as it forced the man to feel and see and hear every awful thing he had done to his child. To know in horrific detail how he made him hurt.

Oliver lashed and kicked and screamed, shaking and swallowing the tainted matter that swarmed around him and inside him.

His hand hit something small and he threw it back, clasping his fingers around it and praying that whatever it was it was a part of the alien that could hear him through her lost and out of control rampage in his mind.

"Please! It hurts me too!" Oliver pulled the thing to his chest, pressing the gentle pulsing heat of it to his skin.

"I know it's bad, and you're really mad." He spoke softly, forced by the fluid of the alien burning his throat and making him hoarse and exhausted. She siphoned him, blind and deaf to his words, and let out another horrid wail in Matthew's face.

"Dindet, I'm sorry, I need—" He choked and coughed, and clenched his tearing eyes shut. "I need you to come back, okay?"

"It hurts me too," Oliver begged her, pressing the warm and round thing into his palms. "...please..stop."

The beast's screeching halted, and it stared at Matthew's horrified face as its attention finally turned to the small and fragile thing inside it that it had sworn to protect.

"Please just come back?" Oliver sobbed, "I don't— I can't see it again. It hurts. It hurts too much."

He clenched the tiny thing in his hands, trembling and aching from the burning of her matter as it fell around him, pressing and pooling into the floor until it congealed and reformed.

"Please...come back." Oliver's voice trembled softly, and he shook his head.

"Oliver..." A hand pressed into his shoulder and he realized the screaming awful noise in his head was gone, replaced by a gentle static only broken by Dindet's words as they whispered among his thoughts.

His eyes fluttered open and the blackness that had clouded his vision was gone. Dindet sat in front of him with a warm and incredibly apologetic smile.

"I'm so—"

Before she had time to react, Matthew's hand cleaved through the alien and he tackled the boy, crashing the bottle in his hand on Oliver's head and slamming him hard into the floor.

All the breath in his lungs left and before he could draw in even the semblance of a gasp, his father's massive hands wrapped tight around his neck and pressed him into the filthy carpet.

"What did you do to me?!" Matthew barked, pulling him up and slamming him hard into the ground as Oliver grappled and struggled underneath him. "You drug me?! Put something in my drink?! YOU FILTHY FUCKING PIECE OF SHIT!"

Oliver made a small squeak of a reply and clawed at the man's face in an attempt to get him off, to let go. Anything.

He could barely see through the blood that seeped into his eyes and tiny pieces of broken glass in the crevices of Matthew's fingers cut into his skin, making it all the harder to focus on just staying alive.

"S-ss" it was barely a hiss let alone a word, but it was enough that Matthew put all his weight onto the child's windpipe, forcing his mouth open in futile effort to suck in air.

Oliver's wide eyes fluttered and his frantic clawing at Matthew's face began to slow until his hands dropped down.

Matthew leaned in close to him, hovering just above him that his rancid breath stung his nostrils.

"I should have killed you the first time."

The man's grip tightened further, and Oliver stared at him in abject horror. Then his eyes grew dull and the world became blurry and cold. He was so tired. All he really wanted to do was go to sleep.

Suddenly Matthew began to tremble, violently, and his hands wrenched themselves away from Oliver's throat, allowing him to regain his senses as a wave of adrenaline hit him. He scrambled back in a fit of hacking coughs as he tried to rebuild precious oxygen.

Oliver drew in a haggard breath and immediately his wild gaze rested on the black-clawed hand that dug into Matthew's head, forcing the man to sit on his knees in shaking paralyzation.

Dindet stood behind him, entirely white as her blackened eyes cracked and fractured around her rage-filled face.

The clown let go of him, but he still sat paralyzed, his eyes wide with a silent terror that etched itself into Oliver's memory.

As Dindet rounded him, placing herself directly between Oliver and his father, she flaked away. Tiny pieces of herself cracking and breaking as they floated and fluttered down like dust to the ground.

"All you do is take," she stated, her voice cold and empty, "take and eat and hurt."

"Hhh- ckk.." Matthew couldn't form words, but his eyes flickered to look at the inhuman thing that had taken complete control of him.

"I'm not the monster," she said, "You are."

Matthew made another noise, and his fingers twitched, but Dindet's glare stayed on him and she raised a clawed hand.

"Now, lay down." The clown lowered her hand slowly, and the man's body cracked and bent in futile effort to resist the demand. He leaned forward, and slowly pressed his face into the carpet.

The moment he had successfully bent to the clown's command, Dindet whipped around and wrapped herself around Oliver, vanishing the both of them from capable sight.

***

Dindet reappeared at the front entrance of the cabin, an enormous black mass that drew Jon's immediate attention. The scientist threw the court papers in his hands aside and scrambled over the couch as she melted away and struggled to hold his beaten and bloodied son.

"Oliver!" His father pulled him out of the alien's grasp and pressed his face into his chest with a gentle but relieved hug. "You're bleeding!"

"I'm alright," Oliver murmured, despite the fact that he couldn't really stand or think straight with the throbbing of his head. "It's not so bad really."

His dad shook his head, gingerly brushing the bloody clump of hair out of Oliver's face. He drew in a breath and grabbed the kid's shoulders, propping him upright enough to get a decent look at the damage.

"I'm taking you to the hospital."

Oliver blinked and his head jerked up, causing him to sway and stumble. "No, you can't!"

"Oliver." Jon's voice was stern, but he followed it up with a sad smile in an attempt to comfort him. "I know you don't want to."

Oliver grabbed his dad's wrists, meekly pulling them away from him and his gaze dropped to the floor, struggling to focus on anything as he wobbled dizzily. "I'm really fine, I'll be okay."

Jon nodded, then shook his head, engulfing the boy in a bear hug. Tight enough that when he stood, he picked him up along with him. "You still need stitches."

"Are..." Oliver hesitated, the thought burned into his mind. The last time he had to go to the hospital. "Are you gonna lie?"

"No, no, no, no." His step-father rested his hand on the boy's head, stroking the matted mess to quell such an awful thought. "I won't do that to you. I won't let him take you back...I should have never let him take you in the first place."

They were really nice words. And Oliver leaned into his dad, his *real* dad, letting his weight fall into him and the kind and gentle embrace he gave.

He missed it. It had only been a couple of days and he missed the way it felt so much and hated that he had already gotten so comfortable with the empty.

He hated that darkness and he hated the way it whispered to him so tenderly, reminding him that those really nice words...were still only words.

Jon pulled away from his son, offering a small smile as if to convey that it was time to go now. Though, Oliver kept his poorly focused eyes on the ground still, only looking up when his father spoke to him.

"You ready to go?"

"No." A stupid simple answer but he really, truly, and honestly didn't want to have to talk to more doctors. Answer their questions about what happened. He wouldn't tell Jon.

Not because an alien clown was involved or anything. But because he was afraid that if he said it, out loud, then it would be real. And he wasn't sure if he could handle that yet.

"I know." Jon patted his back and moved around him, causing Dindet to step out of the way as he moved toward the door. Oliver followed, but before they left Jon turned to Dindet and knelt to meet her at eye level.

"Thank you," he said, staring at her with more relief than she could probably ever understand. Dindet's eyes flickered away from him and she backed up.

"No, really," Jon lay his hand on her shoulder, and she brought her gaze back up to meet him. "Thank you for protecting him."

Rational

liver sat anxiously in front of the television, picking at his fingers and keeping as much attention as he could possibly manage on the badly written paranormal show, so he didn't have to worry about the inevitably terrible news that would follow Jon when he came through the door in an hour or so.

Something justifiably awful, and he knew it, but he didn't want to go to the hearing. He didn't want to go to any of the ones that were probably going to come later, or talk to more counselors, or the protective services, or hear what any of them had to say.

On some level, he was unnervingly calm, almost prepared. It's something he got used to after a while.

He had already begun to succumb to that terrible knowledge that in all likelihood, he would be returned to that monster. He had even thought of how he would go back to what he recognized- at least now, wasn't normal or right by any semblance of the word, and how he might deal with it.

There was a simple, almost gentle familiarity in this, that he was just want to it, or rather to only fall back into it with his eyes shut tight so he could pretend it's not happening at all.

He didn't notice that Dindet had sat down next to him, rolling her legs back and forth to let out the pent-up energy she absorbed from him. She looked different now, dull, and purple like a bruise, and instead of the flower-like paint around her eyes, it had turned to thick shaky squiggles that made her look almost like her face was breaking. Neither of them wanted to talk about what happened.

"Oliver."

"What?!" He barked, jumping at the break of his thoughts and accidentally digging a little too hard into his thumb, slicing it with his nail.

He shot a glare at her, only to be met with worried eyes. "S-sorry."

"It's gonna be okay," she said softly, offering a small smile.

"Shut up." He didn't need or want condolences. Or lies.

Oliver stuck his thumb in his mouth to quell the small sting, refusing to acknowledge her any longer.

The clown lowered her head, looking away, then pulled her knees to her chin in silence, obliging his request despite wanting nothing but to tell him that all she wanted was to help him. But she lost control.

Their silence lasted what felt like hours, long enough that the sun had gone down, but Dindet was sure that was the irregularity of this world.

It was only broken by the ever so quiet sound of the door handle turning, causing Oliver to swivel his head back with a spike of fright before swallowing it all down again as his step-father came inside.

The scientist hung his coat and loosened his tie, quietly taking the keys out of his pocket and hanging them on the key rack as he made his way to his son. He dropped to his knees and engulfed him in a strong, tight hug, like it was the last time he would ever see him, petting his head and squeezing any breath out of the boy as tears rolled down his cheeks and caught in his beard.

"The judge ruled in our favor." Jon's voice trembled, just above a wavering whisper. Oliver shifted in his arms, shock still holding him quiet.

"You're my son." His father's voice nearly cracked, and he held his son's head, kissing his forehead briefly before returning to his almost desperate embrace. "You're not going anywhere."

Oliver let out some small noise, almost like a tearful, relieved half-laugh. His eyes flickered back only for a small second to the clown and the realization hit him.

***

The night was incredibly cold, as the fall usually was, the house was warm though, and even then he couldn't sleep.

Oliver slid the back door open and stared at the dark silhouette of the alien.

"Why did you do it?" His voice was unnervingly calm but he seethed with quiet rage.

The alien cracked and crackled, breaking off pieces of ice as she turned to look at him, her expectant smile dropping immediately and being replaced with a look of guilt as she saw the swirling red and black around him.

"I wanted to help," she answered, standing up as he took a step toward her. *He's mad.*

"I didn't ask for your help." He took another step, forcing her backward and off the porch so he stood over her. "I didn't want your help!"

Why is he so angry?

"You were afraid—" Oliver cut her off with a swipe at her head, forcing Dindet to catch his arm and tear him off balance and into the In-Between in effort to catch him off guard. It didn't work.

"It doesn't matter!" He wrenched his wrist from her grip and stumbled backward with a huff. "I could have dealt with it on my own! I could have—"

For some tiny moment, he searched for words in his irrational rage, shaking his head with impunity. "You can't just DO THAT!!"

He glared at her and her dumbfounded expression as it twisted up in a scowl and she let out a frustrated growl that mirrored his own.

"Why NOT?!" She barked, tearing parts of her hair and hat off and letting them float and circle to reform in a crimson shade. "I just wanted to make it BETTER!"

"I was ready though!" Oliver retorted, "I was used to it, I– I don't need you to screw around with things you don't even get! I can deal with it alone!"

"Ggrrahh! You shouldn't *HAVE TO!*" Dindet stomped and flailed, baring her teeth and beginning to lose herself to her anger. "You keep saying things that don't make ANY SENSE! You have this big black hole in you and you don't let ANYONE DO ANYTHING ABOUT IT!"

Oliver sucked in a breath, taking a hesitant step back as she neared.

She gestured angrily with long blackened claws as she spoke. "It just eats and *eats* at you and you don't even care! Do you have ANY idea how AWFUL IT TASTES?? I just want you to feel better!"

Whatever rage she held began to fade, and she grew smaller until she was standing in front of him sniveling and blue. "I just want you to be happy...you deserve it."

***

A wicked thing, it was.

Oliver sat in his bed, in the dark, hunched up and fuming. Trying to stay as quiet as possible with his gulps and tears and furious, stupid hatred.

The clown brought him back out of the lilac wherever she took him, probably taking advantage of how stupid she left him.

All of it is so, so dumb. He rocked a little, sucking in a hard gasp in effort to force down a burst of loathsome tears.

He was being stupid, and weak, and wrong and he hated every second of it. Hated knowing it.

There was no reason to be so angry. No point in it at all. All she did was solve all your problems but no.

No.

We need to feel hateful and rude and weak.

He was being a fool, choking on his own unfounded rage for no reason, other than that his brain and body, and everything else told him that what was supposed to happen didn't... and that he should feel bad about it. He shouldn't though, obviously.

Oliver wiped a few tears away from his burning face and fell sideways on his bed, dragging in an empty breath that stole almost everything from inside him in one fell swoop.

She was right.

He was just really good at pretending, and for a moment, one very terrible moment, he felt the hole she spoke of. Really and truly felt it.

Something awful and empty and all he was for such a long time. It hurt.

It hurts.

It hurt so much that he had to move and kick and flail in the dark, tearing at all the nothing inside him in order to find some solace that didn't exist, until he couldn't move anymore. A few trembles here and there, and a weight on his chest that bore so deep down he imagined it was the only thing that held him to the earth.

She was right and you were wrong and it hurts.

He wouldn't sleep tonight.

Oliver lay there, staring blankly in the morning. When the sun finally peeked over the trees and made the snow sparkle and glisten, it turned his room a soft orange that bled over the walls onto him and was promptly lost in the hole that never ended.

He thought about more than what an average fourteen-year-old should think about throughout the night.

And came to some conclusion after doubling back and forth on how awful a person he was, to everyone, especially Dindet. Some conclusion that this innocuous event was an opportunity of sorts—one he didn't deserve.

After hours and hours of self-loathing and deliberation over an act of charity that he so righteously refused— and for what? To prove to no one how strong he was in all the wrong ways?

Or rather, just another way to give up.

"Oliver..?" Her voice was small and quiet, causing the boy to sit up and deafly turn his head.

Dindet looked pale and tired, meekly wavering half behind the door as though she was putting in concerted effort to stay whole. She must have been silently warring all night as well.

"I—"

"I'm sorry," Oliver interrupted, hesitant to look at her. The clown hovered in the doorway for a moment, anxiously hanging behind it and still deciding if she should enter.

"You're right." Such a small, tired admission, it rolled off his tongue and left a sour taste in his mouth. Oliver heard her enter, refusing to look at her as she came to sit down next to him on his bed.

He pulled his legs up to his chest, feeling incredibly small in her presence, and vulnerable in a way he didn't like or very well understand. He half expected her to say something, something he would say like; 'yeah, of course, I'm right, why are you so stupid?'

She wasn't like him though, and she didn't speak at all. Only sat there next to him, quietly twiddling her thumbs until she summoned some small courage to wrap an arm around him and pull him closer in a slightly botched hug. She must have imagined that was something human people did when they felt a lot all at once.

Still, though, he was okay with it and sank down, leaning into her and resting his head half on her chest and feeling the very small, fuzzy particles she was made of tickle his cheek.

"I'm so...so sorry."

Epilog

"Mr. Tarsul, the psychologist is in to see you now." A nurse stood in the doorway to the man's hospital room accompanied by a young, incredibly pale woman with bright red hair, holding a blue stress ball in her palm. Matthew sat up in his bed, eyeing the young lady.

"You're gonna say the same damn thing as all the other ones, so I don't get why they sent you here. I wasn't lying about it. I'm not a quack." He croaked, rubbing the back of his neck as she entered.

"Mr. Tarsul, you don't have anything to worry about, I read your files. You can call me Poppy." The woman sat down and unpinned the bright red flower from her shirt, placing it into the man's hand and patiently waiting for the nurse attendant to leave them alone.

"I just have a few questions...about the clown you saw."